SWEET VIOLET'S GHOST

A SWEET COVE MYSTERY BOOK 19

J. A. WHITING

J. A. WHITING BOOKS

To hear about new books and book sales, please sign up for my
mailing list at:
www.jawhiting.com

 Created with Vellum

For everyone who has ever loved a dog

1

It was a warm September afternoon when Angie Roseland and her twin sister, Jenna, pushed their daughters in their strollers up the slight hill near the town park. They followed the winding path under the trees that led to the cemetery at the top of the hill overlooking the ocean. A pleasant breeze rustled the leaves overhead and the sisters chatted about their work days.

Angie and two of her three sisters lived in a Victorian mansion in the seaside town of Sweet Cove, Massachusetts. Jenna lived a couple of houses down on the same street and both young women ran their businesses out of the mansion. Angie's Sweet Dreams Bake Shop was busier than ever even though the summer months had drawn to a close and Jenna, a jewelry designer, had so much work that she was considering hiring an assistant to help out.

"I'm glad you wanted to go for a walk," Jenna told her sister. "Otherwise, I might never come out of my workshop."

"I understand. There's so much going on between our jobs, the babies, community stuff, and everything else." Angie smiled. "But I wouldn't have it any other way."

Almost nine months old, their daughters really weren't babies anymore. Gigi and Libby were born only hours apart and the family kidded that they were as close to being twins as they could be, without being twins.

They emerged from the trees and entered the cemetery where paved pathways crisscrossed the green lawn. The sisters walked to the far side of the peaceful place to look out over the cliff at the glistening ocean stretching far off to the horizon.

"Such a beautiful day." Angie lifted Gigi from the stroller and set her down on the grass with a couple of toys while Jenna did the same with Libby.

The giggling toddlers crawled off together for a few yards.

"These two really seem to be developing fast."

Jenna kept her eye on the girls. "I think they'll be walking soon."

"They're already saying more words than I think is the norm." Angie eyed her sister. "I think having each other makes them try to keep up with one another."

They both looked to their right when they heard Libby babble, "Hi."

Libby was looking across the cemetery where a stonewall separated the old town graveyard from a newer pet cemetery.

Jenna smiled. "Maybe she's talking to the trees." She and Angie returned to their conversation until Gigi said, "Mama. Doggie. Mama."

"Where, hon?" Angie asked glancing around the place. "I don't see a doggie."

Sitting on the grass, Gigi bounced on her butt in excitement. "Doggie, doggie."

Jenna followed the toddler's gaze and her eyes widened. "Huh. What's that?"

"Where?" Angie asked. "What do you see?"

"Oh, gosh." Jenna pointed at the shady entrance to the pet graveyard. "Over there, at the break in the stonewall. At the entrance."

Angie narrowed her eyes as Gigi kept calling out "doggie."

"Can you see the glittering particles?" Jenna asked.

"Oh." Angie's breath caught in her throat.

"It's a ... dog." Jenna was dumbfounded.

Angie looked down at her little daughter, over at the glittering form across the cemetery, and then at her sister. "What is it?"

Jenna's eyes were pinned on the thing sitting near the stonewall. It was clearly wagging its tail at them.

After blinking a few times, Jenna whispered, "I think it's a dog ghost."

"Mama. Doggie." Gigi laughed.

"Yes, hon. You see it?" Angie spun around to Jenna with her mouth open. "Jenna."

It dawned on Jenna why her sister had such a look of shock on her face. "Oh, wow. Gigi can see it. She can see a ghost."

The four Roseland sisters had moved to the seacoast from Boston after Angie inherited the mansion from one of her regular customers, and once settled in town, they'd begun to discover they all had paranormal powers.

"I can't believe it," Angie shook her head. "It's the first time Gigi has shown any abilities."

Libby looked up at her mother with a beaming smile. "Doggie."

Jenna clutched her sister's arm. "Oh, gosh. Libby, too."

The ghost-dog whined a little at them.

Jenna was the family member who often could see ghosts. The others had only ever seen the ghost of their grandmother and most recently, their mother.

"Have you ever seen the ghost of an animal before?" Angie questioned.

Shaking her head, Jenna said, "This is a first."

"If it's a ghost," Angie asked, "why can I see it? I never see ghosts. That's your thing, not mine."

Jenna sighed. "Maybe the ghosts of animals are easier to see."

The dog barked a few times causing the toddlers to laugh with delight.

Jenna reached her hand out to the canine. "Come here. It's okay. Come see us."

They watched in amazement as the small dog trotted across the grass to them, stopped near the little girls, and gave each one a lick on the cheek. Gigi and Libby bounced with joy at the dog's kisses.

The ghost-dog looked like a cross between a Bichon

and a Poodle. It had curly white fur and bright eyes. It wasn't a fully-formed dog … it's body was comprised of glimmering silver, white, and gold particles and appeared as if it was almost see-through. It sat down next to the toddlers and looked up at Jenna and Angie.

"You're a good dog, aren't you?" Jenna spoke to the animal and it wagged its little tail.

"Why is it here?" Angie asked.

"It must have come from one of the graves in the pet cemetery." Jenna kept her eyes pinned on the dog.

"But why now? We come up here all the time. We've never seen her before."

Angie and Jenna slowly turned to one another.

"Is something about to happen that we're going to have to help with?" Jenna's expression was worried.

The look on Angie's face matched her sister's. "Oh. Well, things have been quiet for a while. It's been three months since anything's been going on. I guess it couldn't last forever. I wonder what this is going to be about?"

"Shall we head home? See if she wants to follow us?"

They put the girls in the strollers and started down the pathway back to the town park. Jenna could see that the dog wanted to go along with them.

"Come on. You can come home with us." When she patted her thigh to encourage the canine to join them, the shimmering dog jumped up, darted ahead, stopped to look back, waited, and then trotted along beside the foursome as they went down the hill, through the park, along Main Street to the lane where the mansion stood, all the while wagging its tail.

The Victorian stood set back from the road on a little less than an acre of land with a lovely green lawn, lush trees, and flower gardens put in by Ellie, the middle sister. With more than eighteen rooms, it housed Angie's Sweet Dreams Bake Shop, Jenna's jewelry shop, and a bed and breakfast inn along with rooms for Ellie, Courtney, and Angie, her husband, and daughter. They'd expanded the mansion recently by adding a first floor apartment for Mr. Finch, and there was a large carriage house at the rear of the place that had two two-bedroom apartments on its second floor.

Mr. Finch, an older man who had been lovingly "adopted" by the Roselands and was now an honorary member of their family, sat on the front porch in a rocking chair with a small black cat named Circe on his lap. Euclid, a huge orange Maine Coon cat, was perched on the railing watching Angie, Jenna, and the toddlers come up the walkway to the Victorian ... when he suddenly arched his back and hissed.

"What is it, fine boy?" Finch asked the cat as Circe jumped down to see what had her furry friend on the defensive.

Finch stood and adjusted his black-rimmed eyeglasses as something next to the strollers caught his attention.

"What's this?" Surprise and delight could be heard in the older man's voice when he saw the ghost-dog. "Did you find her in the cemetery?"

Finch bent down to pat the small white, gold, and silver creature and she wagged and wiggled around him. "I can't feel her. It's like putting my hand through the air. But it certainly seems she can feel me patting her."

"We spotted her at the entrance to the pet grave-yard," Angie announced while lifting Gigi from the stroller.

Euclid scowled at the apparition.

"We weren't the first ones to notice the dog." Jenna held Libby on her hip.

Finch looked up at Jenna.

"Gigi and Libby saw her first," Jenna explained.

Right away, Finch moved his eyes from toddler to toddler, and then his face broke into a wide grin. "Well, well. It seems the girls are following in the footsteps of their mothers. How wonderful."

"Doggie." Still held in Angie's arms, Gigi leaned forward trying to touch the new arrival.

Interested in the visitor, Circe went down the steps to sniff at the canine ghost.

"Will she be staying?" Finch smiled. "I always wanted a dog."

Euclid shot the man a look that could kill.

"Oh, my fine boy. There's no need to be angry about someone new. I have more than enough love for all of you." Finch gently ran his hand over the cat's long, orange fur. "You will always hold a special place in my heart, my dear friend. You are irreplaceable."

Euclid's demeanor softened.

Ellie, the middle sister and the one who ran the bed and breakfast inn out of the mansion, came out to the porch with a platter of sugar cookies. "I made extra. How was your walk?"

Angie stepped up onto the porch to get a cookie. She thanked her sister, and then watched to see if Ellie would be able to see the small ghost. After taking a bite, she broke a tiny piece off for Gigi to nibble on.

Ellie was tall with long straight, blond hair, and she was the one who looked most like their deceased mother. Although she was also the sister who was uneasy about their paranormal skills and wished they would disappear, she had strong abilities and had used them in the past to defend her loved ones from harm. More than once, she'd been able to employ telekinesis to disarm a criminal, and she could often tell when something was going to happen before it did.

The sparkling atoms of the ghost dog caught Ellie's eye and she stood gaping at the animal. "What ... what is that?"

"It's a dog," Jenna said matter-of-factly as she helped herself to a cookie. "She followed us home from the cemetery."

"Really? What does she want?" Ellie couldn't peel her eyes from the unusual sight.

"We don't know."

Euclid jumped off the rail and gingerly approached the dog, and after a moment, the two of them touched noses.

Lifting her eyes to her sisters, Ellie asked, "Can everyone see the ghost?"

"We walked through the park and down Main Street on the way home," Angie explained. "No one noticed, so I guess it's just us who can see her."

"Why is she here?" Ellie didn't know what to make of the situation.

Jenna sat down on one of the porch rockers with Libby on her lap. "Maybe she's lonely."

Ellie shot her sister a look of disbelief. "Somehow I think it's more than that." She looked back at the dog. "Do you know her name?"

Angie shook her head. "Maybe she can lead us to her grave in the cemetery. Then we can read her name from the grave marker."

"Why can't this family just be normal?" Ellie said the words mostly to herself.

"Libby and Gigi can see her, too." Finch was full of excitement.

Ellie stared at her nieces. "Their powers are starting very early. This should be interesting." With a sigh and a shake of her head, she turned to go back inside the house. "I'd better put some coffee on. I'll get some squares to add to the cookie platter. Chief Martin loves my peanut butter squares." She disappeared into the Victorian. In addition to her many skills, Ellie almost always could tell when the chief would be coming by for a visit.

"Are you expecting Chief Martin?" Finch asked the sisters.

"No, but here he comes." Jenna gestured to the police car pulling into the driveway.

Angie waved to the man when he emerged from his vehicle. "And so begins another adventure in the Roseland family saga."

2

In his mid-fifties, tall and stocky with a bit of gray in his light brown hair, Chief Phillip Martin had known the Roseland sisters since they were little. The sisters, who grew up in Boston, had visited Sweet Cove every summer staying with their nana in her small cottage on Robin's Point. The sisters' grandmother had powerful paranormal abilities and she was called in often by the police to help on cases, and she and Chief Martin had been close friends.

"Afternoon," the chief nodded. "How's everyone doing?"

Euclid and Circe hurried to greet him and they received petting that resulted in loud purring.

Angie watched the man's face to see if he noticed

the ghost dog, but the chief seemed to look right through the canine without any acknowledgment.

"We're good," Jenna told him. "Angie and I just came back from a walk with the girls."

"Nice day for it."

"Ellie's making coffee. She'll be right out," Angie said. "Have a seat?"

"I'd love to." The chief settled on the rocker next to Finch and let out a deep breath.

"Long day?" Finch asked their friend.

"Some seem a lot longer than others," the chief admitted. Circe jumped on his lap and he stroked the cat's black fur.

Ellie emerged from the house with a tray holding cups, a coffee pot, creamer and sugar, and a plate of cookies and squares. She set it down on a small wooden side table and poured the coffee for everyone.

"Exactly what I needed." The chief took a long swallow of his black coffee and leaned back in his chair.

The little ghost dog sat at the man's feet and stared up at him with interest.

"Ellie knew you were coming," Jenna said.

The chief wasn't surprised. He knew about Ellie's ability to sense when he was coming to the house.

"No, I didn't. I had no idea he was coming." Ellie held the cookie plate so the chief could make his selection, and he took one of the peanut butter squares.

Angie shook her head and whispered. "Yes, she did."

"What brings you by, Phillip?" Finch asked with a smile. "Is it purely a social call?"

"As a matter of fact," the chief said, "it isn't."

Courtney, the youngest sister, came down the street and turned onto the walkway to the front porch. She and Finch co-owned the candy store on Main Street. Courtney had long honey-blond hair and blue eyes and looked very much like Angie. When people discovered Angie had a twin, they mistakenly thought it was Courtney.

"Hey, everyone, what's cookin'?" The young woman went up the steps to the porch and took one of the squares from the plate. "You'd think I'd be tired of sweets from working in a candy store all day, but somehow I'm not." Her eyes widened when she spotted the shimmering dog at Chief Martin's feet. "What's this?"

A surprised expression washed over the chief's face as he stared at Courtney wondering why she looked so shocked to see him.

Angie said, "Chief Martin just got here. We haven't had a chance to talk to him about our new guest."

"There's a new guest at the B and B I should know about?" he asked.

"No, it isn't that. I'll explain to both of you." Angie leaned against the porch railing and told them how she and Jenna met the spirit dog while walking in the cemetery.

"That's so cool." Courtney smiled as she knelt beside the sparkling dog and reached out to pat her. "Huh, I can't feel her, but she sure can feel my hand on her."

"Can you see the dog, Phillip?" Finch asked.

"I can't." The chief squinted to see if narrowing his eyes would sharpen his vision. "What if you put a collar on her? Then I'd know where she was by seeing the collar moving around."

One of Angie's eyebrows shot up at the suggestion. "Maybe we could try that, but it could cause some problems if the B and B guests saw a collar floating around in mid-air."

Courtney laughed at the mental image. "Maybe we can do that closer to Halloween."

The little dog wagged her tail.

"Wait a second," Courtney said. "How come all

of us can see the dog? Except for Chief Martin, I mean. None of us can usually see spirits. That's Jenna's territory. Jenna's the one who can see ghosts, not us."

Jenna shrugged. "It could be that the rest of you just can't see *human* ghosts?"

After more discussion about the new ghost and speculation about why all the Roseland sisters and Mr. Finch could see the dog, Finch changed the subject.

"Phillip, do you need something from us? Right before Miss Courtney came home, you mentioned that your visit wasn't only for social reasons. Is everything all right?"

All eyes turned to the chief.

"No, it isn't." The man let out a sigh. "There's a situation on the edge of town over by Silver Cove. I wondered if some of you could come take a look around."

"What's going on over there?" Courtney asked. "I haven't seen anything on Twitter."

"That's a good thing, but I don't expect that to last much longer. The crime scene investigators are there right now. We've been working hard to keep this quiet in order to process the scene without interruption from the media and people gathering to gawk. We were called to the house early this morning. The mail carrier reported that a couple days of mail had built up, but that the homeowner's car was parked in the driveway. The mail carrier rang the doorbell, but no one answered. After an officer did a wellness check, we all descended on the place."

Anxiety pinged through Angie's body and Euclid let out a low hiss.

No one asked the chief any questions so as not to interrupt as he shared the preliminary information with them.

"A woman owns the house. Her name is Rachel Princeton. Do any of you know her?" The chief looked at the sisters and each one shook her head. "She's lived there for about two years. There are signs of a struggle inside the house. There's some blood. The woman is missing. Law enforcement in the area have been notified and are on the lookout for her."

"If she left the house on her own," Jenna suggested, "and she was injured, she might not have gotten too far."

Chief Martin nodded. "There's been a preliminary search conducted in the woods around the property. Local hospitals have been contacted. So far, nothing."

"Do you know anything else about the woman?" Angie questioned.

"Ms. Princeton is an architect. She works from home fairly frequently. She travels for work on occasion. There's a sister in New Hampshire. She's on her way down." The chief directed his question to Ellie. "Do you happen to have a room available? I suggested the sister get in touch with you."

"We had a cancellation this morning," Ellie told the man. "I can set it aside for her."

"Thank you. Ms. Princeton is around thirty. Not sure about friends or if she has a partner. She lives alone." The chief paused for a few seconds. "Would any of you be able to take a ride over there? Take a look around?"

"Now?" Angie asked.

The chief nodded. "If you can."

"I'll go, if someone can watch Gigi."

"I'll be happy to stay with the girls," Finch offered.

"Could you get Orla to come over?" the chief asked. "I'd like to have your insight, Mr. Finch." The man looked at the sisters. "I'd like as many of you to come along as possible. I know you're probably busy, Ellie." Chief Martin knew Ellie would prefer not to see the active crime scene.

"I'll call Orla." Jenna stood and removed her phone from her sweater pocket. She handed Libby to Finch, and went inside to place the call. Orla Abel was a family friend who lived in the house behind the Victorian with her husband Mel, and babysat the children each week when Finch went to work.

"What about the cats?" Angie asked.

"If it's not too much trouble, it wouldn't hurt to have them there." The chief glanced around the porch. "What about the new ghost?"

"We'll bring her, if she wants to come along," Angie said.

The dog stood and walked down the porch steps to wait on the front lawn.

"It seems she's willing to go with us." Angie had noticed that the dog had been subdued while the chief reported the news of the recent crime. She knew the ghost dog was most likely linked to the case in some way. The timing was too perfect.

Rachel Princeton's home was an old, well-tended white house with a wrap-around porch set back from the street with a long driveway that led to a detached two-car garage. Police cars and an ambulance parked along the drive, and several people hurried back and forth from the house to a couple of the police vans.

Angie and Jenna got out of Jenna's car and opened the rear doors to let out the cats and ghost dog. Courtney and Finch had ridden with the chief, and she helped the older man from the vehicle and handed him his cane.

They all stood quietly for a few moments facing the house, steeling themselves to what they were about to see.

What happened here? Angie looked down at the little spirit at her feet, and the dog met her gaze with sad, sad eyes.

3

An officer spotted the chief and hurried over to converse with him in hushed tones. The police officer took a look at the cats, but didn't ask anything about why they were there.

"We can go in," Chief Martin told them. "You know the drill. Don't touch anything. See what you can pick up on. There are still some investigators in the house, but the forensic evidence has been collected already. Ready?"

"Should the cats wait in the car?" Angie asked.

"Could they sniff around the property?" the chief inquired. "See if they pick up on any scents?"

"They can do that." Angie explained to the felines that they would be going inside the house, but if either of them needed anything, they should meow at the door. "Okay, we're all set."

The chief led the way to the backdoor of the home. It was open so he guided his friends into the back hall and then to the kitchen. "I won't say anything about the preliminary findings until you're done. I don't want to influence your impressions. Go ahead and walk around."

The family members separated and went their own ways walking slowly through the rooms.

Angie had to suck in her breath and close her eyes when she saw the blood on the kitchen wall. She kept her eyes on the floor and entered the living room where she moved about the space trying to pick up anything that floated on the air.

She walked through the dining room, a sitting room, a library that seemed to have been used as an office, a first floor bedroom, and a bath. Upstairs there were four more bedrooms and two baths, and there was an unfinished attic on the third floor. Returning to the main floor, Angie walked back into the large living room and spotted the ghost dog sitting next to the fireplace.

"What's going on here, little one? Did you know Rachel Princeton?"

The dog moved her eyes to the mantle and Angie followed her gaze.

"Oh." Some photos in silver frames were set on the mantle and one in particular caught her eye. A woman with long brown hair smiled at the camera. She sat on a log in the woods with a small white dog next to her. The woman had her arm around her companion.

Angie spotted a purple dog collar placed next to the photograph. One word was embroidered along the length of the band. *Violet.*

Some tears gathered in her eyes as she looked down at the ghost dog. "Violet," she whispered. "You were Rachel's dog. She loved you, didn't she?"

Little Violet stared into Angie's eyes and the young woman's heart contracted with sorrow.

"Angie?" Jenna walked over to her sister. "Are you done?" She noticed the expression on her sister's face. "What's wrong?"

Angie gestured to the photo and the dog collar on the mantle.

"Oh, I see. It's our new friend in the picture. She used to belong to Rachel." Jenna turned to the dog. "This was your house, right? Do you know where Rachel is?"

Violet took a quick look to the kitchen, but didn't move from her spot sitting next to the sisters.

Courtney and Mr. Finch, leaning on his cane, walked into the room and Angie showed them the things on the mantle.

"So Violet died before Rachel's disappearance," Courtney thought aloud.

"But somehow the dog knew the woman was in trouble and came to Angie and Jenna for help," Finch surmised.

"Shall we go outside and talk?" Jenna suggested. Although the house was large, it was feeling tight and cramped with all the officers and investigators coming and going.

Once outside, the sisters and Finch found the cats on the patio and they sat down to discuss what they'd all sensed.

"I ran my hand over the kitchen counter," Finch told them. "I picked up on feelings of surprise, fear, regret. There was a chaotic atmosphere in the kitchen. I assume someone came in through the rear door and accosted Ms. Princeton. I felt the remnants of a fight. I believe Ms. Princeton was still alive when she was taken from the house."

"Wow, Mr. Finch," Courtney marveled at the man. "You were able to pick up a lot. I felt traces of fear and desperation, but nothing so fully formed as what you sensed."

"So you think Rachel was taken? She didn't leave or escape on her own?" Angie questioned.

"That is correct, Miss Angie."

Jenna asked, "Does anyone feel something that can tell us if Rachel is still alive? Can any of you feel her energy? Is her spirit still here or has it gone?"

"I don't feel anything either way," Courtney offered.

The others agreed.

"That might be a good sign," Finch told them. "At least, we don't feel that her energy is floating away on its own. She may still be alive."

"There's an awful lot of blood in the kitchen," Angie said. "I wonder if her wounds are fatal."

"What about Violet?" Jenna asked. "Does she sense anything about her owner?"

Violet sat off to the side listening, but she didn't react to Jenna's question.

"And what about our fine feline friends?" Finch asked as he looked to the cats sitting on one of the patio chairs. "Euclid, Circe ... did you discover anything on your inspection of the grounds?"

The cats leapt from the chair and disappeared around the corner of the house.

The sisters and Finch hurried after them and found the animals near the garage. The sun had nearly set and darkness gathered around the house. A motion detector floodlight came on when the family members got closer to the building.

Violet appeared next to the cats and she sniffed all around the ground in front of the garage. She stopped and pawed at the soil.

Chief Martin spotted the small group and strode across the lawn toward them. "Anything? Did you pick up on anything?"

Angie glanced around and noticed a small compact sedan parked in the driveway closer to the house. "Is that Rachel's car over there?"

"That's right," the chief said. "The mail carrier reported that the car hasn't moved from that spot for three days."

"Remember we had that downpour the other night?" Angie asked. "It was a few days ago. See what the cats are looking at? The ghost dog's name is Violet. She's next to the cats."

Chief Martin moved to where the cats were staring at the ground. He leaned down and looked at the spot of soil just off the driveway where the grass had died over the hot summer. "There's a tire print here. It isn't from Ms. Princeton's car. It's a truck tire."

The chief stood straight. "I don't think it belongs to a mail truck either. I'll get the team on it. They can take the image and determine what make of vehicle it belongs to. The print must have been made right after the rain storm we had the other day. It would have been muddy then. Good work, everyone."

"It was Euclid, Circe, and Violet who found it," Jenna pointed out.

"Good work, cats." The chief smiled at the felines, then glanced around for the ghost. "Good work, Violet, wherever you are."

The family told the chief what they'd felt when they were in the house.

"Okay, good. Mr. Finch, you believe Ms. Princeton was alive when she left the house. I guess I should say *taken* from the house. Let's hope she's still alive, and we can find her fast."

Finch asked, "You're the experienced one, Phillip. What are the odds that Ms. Princeton is still alive?"

The chief's face darkened. "We think she attacked three days ago. Based on the amount of blood in the house and the fact she's been missing for several days, I'm sorry to say the odds aren't good. Not good at all."

～

Back at the Victorian, Angie found her husband, Josh, napping on the sofa with Gigi asleep in his arms. When she sat down next to him, he woke up and smiled at her.

"We decided to take a snooze," he whispered, and then leaned in to kiss her.

"Have you eaten?"

"I fed Gigi, but waited to have dinner with all of you. Is everyone back now?" Josh asked. "Was the woman found?"

"Not yet. The crime scene was ... a mess."

"I'm sorry you had to see that." Josh's eyebrows scrunched together. "Where's that light coming from?"

"What light?"

"Something's shining on the rug. It's all sparkly. Right over there." Josh pointed.

Angie looked to where her husband indicated and saw Violet sitting there. With her heart starting to race, she turned quickly to Josh. "What kind of light is it?"

"Um. Sparkly."

Gigi blinked her eyes open and looked across the room. "Doggie."

"What doggie, honey?" Josh asked. "There's no

dog there." Then he looked at his wife with wide eyes. "Is there?"

"There is." Angie nodded, and explained about the ghost dog. Her face was full of excitement. "Her name is Violet. Josh, you can see her. Not completely, but you're able to see her shimmering. This is amazing. You can see a ghost."

Josh looked at the place on the rug where the dog was still sitting. He moved his eyes to Angie, and then back to the dog. "I can see her sparkles."

A wide smile spread over Angie's face. "Josh, you can see her. You can see her spirit."

Josh didn't say anything for several seconds. "But how can I?"

The front door of the Victorian opened and Rufus Fudge, Courtney's boyfriend, walked into the foyer. He saw Angie, Josh, and Gigi sitting on the sofa and went into the living room to say hello.

Rufus stopped and trained his gaze on the rug. "What's that? Where's that weird light coming from?"

"Oh, gosh," Angie whispered. "I'd better go get Courtney."

4

"Courtney's in the kitchen." Angie hurried over to Rufus. "Josh is trying to get Gigi to nap," she fibbed trying to distract the young man from the unusual light on the rug.

Rufus followed Angie across the foyer and down the hall to the kitchen. "Courtney texted me. She told me all of you were with Chief Martin at a crime scene."

"We went together. We just got back."

Jenna and Ellie stood at the counter working on some side dishes to go with the Shepherd's pies baking in the ovens, and Circe and Euclid were sitting on top of the refrigerator watching the goings-on.

"Hey." With a big smile, Courtney walked over to

Rufus and gave him a kiss before returning to the kitchen island. "I'm making a salad to go with dinner."

"I'll help you in a second." Rufus went to the coffee bar to pour himself a hot drink.

Angie whispered to her sister, "He could see Violet's shimmering particles."

Courtney tilted her head as a look of astonishment washed over her face. "Well, that's interesting."

"Josh can see them, too. You'll have to tell him soon." Angie meant that her sister would need to have a talk with her boyfriend to explain about the family's paranormal powers. He was the only one of the boyfriends and husbands who hadn't yet been told. Courtney had been putting it off, afraid it might chase him away.

"What's interesting?" Rufus asked his girlfriend as he sipped the hot coffee.

Courtney and Angie exchanged quick looks.

"The case we were at today," Courtney told him. "We can't say much about it since it's an active investigation."

"It's all over social media." Rufus sat on a stool next to the counter. "Has the woman been found?"

"Not yet." Courtney slid some vegetables over the

counter and handed her boyfriend a knife. "Would you cut these up to put in the salad?"

"Sure thing." Rufus was an Englishman who had come to Sweet Cove to work with Jack Ford, Ellie's boyfriend, in his law office.

Jenna's husband, Tom, walked into the kitchen carrying a bottle of wine and a pack of craft beer. "Hi all. I found this guy outside skulking around," he kidded and gestured to Jack Ford who was right behind him. Jack wore a starched shirt and his usual bow tie. This one was navy blue with red dots.

"I was doing no such thing." Jack placed a container of homemade ice cream on the table. He looked over at Rufus. "How did you get here so quick? Did you skip out of the office early?"

"You're just slow. Anyway, I'm younger than you. That makes me faster." Rufus didn't look up from cutting the vegetables.

"Maybe it's time to reduce your salary," Jack muttered to Jack as he went over to give Ellie a hug.

Jenna took the beer from her husband and put it in the refrigerator. "Libby okay?"

"Orla's with her. She's just putting her down," Tom said.

The last person to arrive was Finch's girlfriend, Betty Hayes, a highly successful Sweet Cove real estate broker. Carrying a pumpkin bread, the woman bustled into the kitchen like a whirlwind. "Am I late? It smells good in here. I was with the most difficult client. There's something wrong with everything I show her. It's becoming ridiculous. You can't have perfection, for goodness sake. Buy something and make it your own." She hurried over to Finch and smothered him in a hug, pulling the side of his head into her ample bosom. "But now that I see my sweetheart, Victor, my stress is melting away." Standing over Finch, she kissed him on the head several times. "Such a perfect man."

Finch blushed at the woman's attention.

Josh came into the kitchen and greeted everyone. "Can I set the table? Gigi's asleep in the playpen in the sunroom."

Knowing it was Josh's favorite brand, Tom opened a beer and handed it to his brother-in-law. "Come on, I'll help you with the table." When the men headed for the dining room, the cats jumped down and took off after them.

The food and drinks were brought to the table and everyone took their seats. The cats perched on the top of the tall dining hutch, but Violet was nowhere to be seen. Angie thought the dog stayed out of sight because people other than the sisters and Mr. Finch could see her sparkles.

"Have you heard about the missing woman?" Betty passed the basket of cornbread to Mr. Finch.

Angie nodded. "We did hear."

Finch patted the woman's hand. "In fact, Chief Martin asked some of us to visit the crime scene and give our impressions."

Betty's jaw dropped. "Why does he think you can help? I don't understand it. Why does he ask for your help so often?"

Tom spoke up. "Mr. Finch and the Roseland sisters are very observant. They notice things that others miss. They're also very logical and have strong reasoning skills. That combination has proven to be very helpful to the police."

Circe trilled from the top of the cabinet.

"Aren't the officers well-trained in those skills?" Rufus added some wine to his glass. "Why do they need civilians to assist?"

"They are well-trained," Courtney explained. "But there are times when fresh eyes on a crime scene can discover things that were overlooked."

"I sold her that house, you know." Betty took a sip from her water glass.

"Who do you mean?" Angie questioned.

"The missing woman. Rachel Princeton. She seemed like a nice person. Nothing like this new client of mine." Betty rolled her eyes. "It makes me shudder to think Rachel has been harmed. And right inside her own home, too. The home I sold to her. What's happening to the world?"

"Crimes have been committed for thousands of years," Jack said. "But news travels like lightning now. We hear of bad things happening all over the world and in a matter of minutes."

Betty sighed. "Who would want to hurt that young woman?"

"What do you know about her?" Jenna asked.

Betty said, "She's an architect. Her employer is located in Boston, but the architects could work from home. Once in a while, Rachel goes into the city for meetings. She wanted to live in a small town near the seacoast."

"Did she have a partner?" Finch questioned.

"She didn't. Not at the time. She wanted to make an investment in real estate, but she wanted a cozy home with some land and with easy access to the ocean. She fell in love with that house." Betty shook her head. "If only she knew what was going to happen in there. She would have chosen somewhere else to live."

"Did Rachel have any pets?" Jenna glanced at Angie before turning her attention to Betty from across the table.

"Pets?" Betty's face brightened. "Why yes, she did. A small delightful dog. I believe her name was Violet. She was one of the few animals I've met that I liked."

Euclid hissed.

Betty waved her hand toward the cabinet. "Oh, Euclid. Don't take everything so personally." She shook her head. "Why am I addressing the cat? He doesn't know what I'm saying."

Finch smiled up at the orange cat and exchanged a knowing look with him.

"What about family? Did Rachel mention any family?" Jenna asked.

Betty tapped at her chin, thinking. "Family, hmm, I don't recall. I believe she grew up in New Hampshire, but I might be confusing her with someone else." After a few seconds, Betty added, "Yes, I remember now. She did grow up in New Hampshire. Rachel told me there were more professional opportunities in Boston so she wanted to live within thirty minutes of the city because she had to go into the office once or twice a week. She also traveled for business and didn't want to be too far from Logan Airport."

"How long ago did you sell the house to her?" Courtney reached for an extra helping of Shepherd's pie.

"Oh, let me think. I usually remember such things. It was two years ago, in the summer. She's been living in the house for a little over two years."

"It's kind of a big place for only one person," Courtney noted. "I wonder why she didn't want something smaller."

"Rachel loved the house, the location, and the privacy the lot afforded," Betty said.

"Have you seen Rachel recently?" Tom asked.

"No, maybe a year ago. I ran into her at the market. Her little dog had passed away. She was feeling very low about it."

"What happened to the dog?" Ellie questioned.

"Diabetes." Betty sighed heavily. "I didn't even know dogs could have diabetes. She buried her little friend in the town pet cemetery. I thought that was touching."

Angie noticed Violet sitting in the foyer listening to the conversation. Her glowing particles seemed a little less bright. *Maybe Violet is trying not to be seen.*

Circe leapt down from the cabinet and padded

over to the ghost dog where she gently sniffed her, and then sat down next to her.

Angie smiled at Circe for being kind to the dog.

"Why don't we clear away the dishes and bring out coffee, tea, and dessert?" Josh suggested.

Everyone started to get up, but Josh told the women and Mr. Finch that they'd prepared the dinner so he, Tom, Rufus, and Jack would do the cleanup.

Angie went to the sunroom to check on Gigi and found her sound asleep. She tucked the soft flannel blanket around the little girl's shoulders before heading back to the dining room.

A pie, a cheesecake, and Betty's pumpkin bread were on the side table along with the homemade ice cream Jack had made, and Ellie was plating the desserts and serving everyone at the table. Courtney poured tea and coffee for whoever wanted it.

Jenna went to the kitchen to get some more napkins and when she returned, she was carrying Angie's phone. "You had a call from Chief Martin." She handed the phone to her sister. "It ended before I could get to it."

Adrenaline rushed through Angie's veins as she excused herself from the table and went to Ellie's office to return the call.

The others chatted together, but each one wondered what the chief wanted.

In a few minutes, Angie was back in the dining room. She looked at her sisters and Finch. "The chief wants us to come help him with something. There's been a report that Rachel Princeton was seen walking near the highway."

5

It was dark when Angie, Jenna, Courtney and Mr. Finch met Chief Martin at Rachel Princeton's house. They didn't go inside, but stood in the driveway to speak with the chief.

"Two different people called the tip line saying they saw someone of Rachel's description walking near the highway. One caller reported seeing blood on a woman."

"It must be her," Courtney's voice sounded excited.

"I don't want to dampen any enthusiasm," the chief told them, "but when a request goes out to the public about a missing person, we get a lot of calls and some of them are off the wall. If the person who called today saw someone who looked like Rachel and saw blood on her, why didn't the person stop to offer help? Or at least keep her in sight until an officer could get there."

"I see your point," Courtney nodded. "You get a lot of false sightings from nuts and crazies."

"We get enough of them, yes," the chief said. "So I'm skeptical. It is worth looking into though. We may get lucky. There are a number of officers patrolling around this end of town looking for Rachel. It's dark and it will be very difficult to see. I asked you to come because I thought you might be able to sense which way to go. I also thought it might be helpful to meet here at the house ... maybe being here might rev up your abilities. You know, like priming a pump. I really don't know what I'm talking about. Do you feel anything?"

"Let us walk around for a few minutes," Angie suggested. "Maybe we'll feel something."

"Okay. Before you wander off, the tire print you found in the dirt was from an F-150 truck. That's helpful to know, but the F-150 is the most sold vehicle in the United States. Last year alone, almost a million of those trucks were sold."

"So, not helpful," Jenna said.

"We're trying to find out if there were any deliveries

made here over the past several days ... supplies for some project, or maybe an electric company worker here to read a meter, a town property assessor looking around. Things like that. So far, there aren't any links. We've talked to a couple of the neighbors. They didn't notice anything out of the ordinary, but there's a long driveway leading to the house so no one might have noticed a truck back here." The chief took off his hat and ran his hand through his hair. "Anyway, take your walk around and let's see if you sense anything."

Courtney and Finch wandered off behind the house while Angie and Jenna stayed in front.

"Do you think someone really saw Rachel on the road?" Jenna used a flashlight and stayed close to Angie.

"Probably not. It seems unlikely. Stranger things have happened though." Angie held a flashlight, too, as they walked slowly around the yard in front of the house.

Fifteen minutes passed and Angie hadn't picked up on a single thing. "I'm not having any luck. I feel like there's something blocking me. Not much moving freely on the air."

"Yeah, I haven't felt or seen anything that could be related to a paranormal phenomenon," Jenna agreed. "Shall we get out on the road to look for Rachel?"

"Why not. No time like the present."

The sisters spoke to the chief before heading to Jenna's car. Chief Martin told them he'd call when Courtney and Mr. Finch came back and they were driving around. "Divide and conquer. Once we're in the car, I'll have Courtney call your cell phone. That way we can advise each other about what we're seeing, or not seeing."

"Sounds like a good idea," Angie agreed. "We'll head toward the highway where the callers reported seeing Rachel."

Jenna pulled out of the driveway and turned in the direction of the highway.

"It's so dark." Angie watched out the window. "I don't know if this is going to work. If Rachel was just a couple of feet into the woods, we'd never be able to see her. But if she stands still directly under a street-lamp and waves at us, then maybe we'll notice her," Angie kidded.

"Or maybe not," Jenna deadpanned.

"Do you feel we should go in a certain direction?" Angie asked.

"I don't, do you?"

"No."

"Here's a different topic that's been on my mind," Jenna said as she made a turn. "Why can people who have never seen a single paranormal thing, suddenly see a ghost dog?"

Angie smiled. "I have no idea. Josh was baffled by it, and it made him sort of uneasy. He doesn't know how to deal with it."

"Sort of like all of us," Jenna kidded as she turned the car on the road that ran parallel to the highway. "Remember how odd it all felt when our skills were just starting?"

"I sure do. It almost made me feel like I could be losing my mind. It was a weird mix of excitement and dread. I feel an obligation to use my skills to help, to be useful, to do some good. But I'm always sure I'm going to mess up."

Jenna agreed. "And I wish they'd be more consistent. Sometimes, I feel really sharp and that I'm in control, but other times, I feel like I'm fumbling around in the dark."

The sky was overcast blocking out any light from the moon and stars. "You mean like right now?" Angie grinned as she looked out into the dark night.

"Yes, literally and figuratively."

Angie's phone buzzed with an incoming call from Courtney.

"What's cookin'?" she asked.

"Not a whole lot." Angie told her sister where they were. "We haven't seen anyone who looks like Rachel."

"We're driving along the country roads around Rachel's house," Courtney reported. "Then we'll follow the road to the beach. I don't feel anything and neither does Mr. Finch."

"Too bad. I was hoping you were having more luck than we are."

After an hour of driving around, the mission was ended and Jenna and Angie rendezvoused with the chief, Courtney, and Mr. Finch. They discussed the probability of Rachel walking around, injured and disoriented.

"The young woman would most likely have waved someone down," Finch guessed. "Or she might have passed out and someone would have seen her. She could be in the woods, however."

"Officers and dogs will search the woods tomorrow. Maybe we'll get lucky," the chief said. "Thanks for coming out. It was worth a shot."

Jenna brought Angie, Courtney, and Mr. Finch home and then she went inside with them for a few minutes.

Mr. Finch was tired and wished the sisters good night before he headed to his apartment.

Ellie was eager to hear the news, and she deflated when she heard nothing had come of the search. "I've been sitting here reading. The ghost dog was with me for most of the evening. She seems very sweet."

"Where is she now?" Courtney asked.

"She left the room a few minutes ago with Circe. They're around here somewhere." Ellie looked at Courtney. "You need to have a chat with Rufus. He could see Violet's particles. You should tell him."

Courtney's shoulders slumped. "I know. It's just so hard to start a conversation like that."

The three sisters explained how they'd told their partners.

"I was a nervous wreck," Jenna said. "I was sure Tom would think we were all crazy. I thought he'd reject me. But he didn't. He was intrigued and wanted to know everything about it."

"Josh thought it was amazing," Angie recalled. "He thought all of us were incredible." She smiled, and teased. "Especially me."

"Jack was his usual analytical self. He told me he wasn't surprised to hear we had paranormal skills. It all made sense," Ellie said. "I think he'd suspected something was different with all of us."

"How do you think Rufus will take it when I tell him?" Courtney asked.

"I know he's smart, and he must know there's more to the world than our five senses tell us there is," Angie said thoughtfully. "Don't underestimate his ability to believe in what he can't see."

Courtney took in a slow, deep breath. "I'll tell him. Tomorrow."

Angie decided to go up to her rooms. She tried to be quiet while she changed into her pajamas so she wouldn't wake Josh. She slipped into Gigi's room to check on her, and for a few minutes, she stood by the crib and watched her little one sleep, then she went to the living room and sat down trying to unwind before heading to bed.

It seemed like finding the ghost dog at the cemetery was weeks ago, but it had only been that afternoon. She thought about Rachel and what could have happened to her, and her heart sank with sadness.

A sparkling light caught her eye and she looked up to see Violet sitting on the floor by one of the easy chairs.

"Are you okay, Violet?"

The dog's little tail hit the floor.

"We're trying to figure out what happened to Rachel. It will take some time. As Mr. Finch always says, we haven't been foiled by a case yet. We'll do our best. I promise you that."

Violet's tail bumped the floor.

Angie tapped the cushion of the sofa with her hand. "Want to sit with me?"

The glittering particles moved across the room, and the ghost jumped up and sat next to Angie. She patted the dog, and despite feeling nothing but air, Violet appeared to enjoy the petting.

"Do you know where Rachel is?" Angie asked.

Violet only stared.

"Do you know if she's alive?"

Again, Violet just blinked.

"It's okay. I know you understand that Rachel is in trouble and that's why you came to us for help. We'll all figure it out together."

Violet closed her eyes and snuggled next to Angie.

"Good dog. You're a sweet one, Violet."

Angie kept patting the little ghost until her own eyes closed, and in just a few minutes, the two of them were sound asleep.

6

The next morning, the bake shop was busy with customers and many of the conversations among the locals centered on Rachel Princeton's disappearance. Angie and her employees buzzed behind the counter preparing coffees, teas, protein drinks, and smoothies while also serving people sitting at the counter, at the tables, and in the takeout line.

Francine, a friend of the sisters and a stained-glass artist with shops on Main Street and in Silver Cove, sat at one of the small tables near the windows. Angie brought her a coffee and a blue-berry muffin and sat down with her for a few minutes.

"I know Rachel Princeton. Not well, but we'd met a few times. She lives not far from me. I couldn't believe it when I heard the news." Francine reached for the coffee mug and took a quick swallow. "You're friends with Chief Martin. Does he have any news? Are there any clues about what happened to the woman?"

Angie shook her head. "Not yet. It seems she went missing about two or three days before police were called to the house, so that didn't help the investigation."

"Why were the police called? What triggered the concern?"

"The mail carrier noticed Rachel hadn't taken in the mail for a few days," Angie explained.

"She lived alone obviously," Francine said.

"It seems so. We heard Rachel is an architect for a firm in Boston."

"Yeah, that's right. Rachel is very successful. She gives talks all around the country on preservation and restoration. She's taught at universities in the area. She knows a lot about moving antique houses from one place to another and she's managed some important restoration projects, too. I believe she's written a couple of books."

"I didn't know that. She's young to have made such a name for herself already."

"Do you think her success had something to do

with her going missing?" Francine wore a concerned look on her face.

"How do you mean?"

"Could someone have been jealous of her success? A rival architect, maybe?"

"That's an interesting theory," Angie thought about the possibility. "How did you meet her?"

"Her property straddles the Silver Cove and Sweet Cove town line. Rachel was at some of the historical society's meetings and some fundraisers held in town. She seems very civic minded and interested in being involved in the community." Francine clutched her mug. "I've heard people say blood was found at the scene. Why would someone kidnap her? That's what happened, right?"

Angie said, "I assumed that was the most likely situation, but it's not necessarily what happened."

"What else could it have been?" Francine looked confused.

"Maybe she tried to end her life, got scared, changed her mind, became disoriented, and left the house," Angie explained one of the possibilities.

"They did a search for her yesterday. If that was the cause, wouldn't they have found her by now? Wouldn't she have turned up at a hospital?"

"Probably. I just don't know."

"What other ideas do you have?"

"Someone she knew could have come by the house and for some reason, they got into a fight. Maybe the person removed the body and buried her somewhere."

Francine cringed at the thought. "None of the possibilities are good ones. I wonder if it was random or planned. Was it someone she knew or a stranger? Maybe someone made a delivery to the house and attacked her. I'm glad I'm not an investigator. I couldn't handle things like this. I wouldn't want to be responsible for solving the crime."

Angie had thoughts like that many times since she'd started helping Chief Martin.

The line at the counter was growing so Angie stood. "Nice to see you. We all need to get together for dinner one of these days."

"You all stay safe," Francine said.

"You, too."

As she was approaching the counter, a woman spoke to Angie.

"Would you make me a protein drink? The drink always makes me feel better when you make it."

Angie smiled at Tori Brothers. The woman was in her forties and owned a cleaning service. Her husband had recently passed away and Angie knew she was struggling.

"You bet I will. What flavor would you like today?"

"Bananas and cream." Tori sat on a counter stool that had just been vacated.

"How's business?" Angie took out the ingredients she would need to make the shake.

"It's going pretty well. I have good clients."

"How are the kids doing?"

"I'm keeping them busy and they're back in school now so that helps."

Tori had two daughters, ten and twelve. They'd taken the death of their father very hard.

Angie concentrated for a minute while she blended the ingredients together. One of her special skills was the ability to put *intention* into whatever food or drink she made. When she'd first met Josh and Mr. Finch, Angie had daydreamed about her feelings for Josh while she was baking, and when Finch ate one of the muffins, it caused him to fall in love with her. Luckily, the spell was temporary, but Angie learned an important lesson that day. She had to be very careful with her thoughts when she was preparing food.

Knowing that Tori was depressed over the loss of

her husband and overwhelmed by her circumstances, Angie tried to put positive thoughts into
whatever she made for the woman. Today, as she
mixed and blended the protein shake, she funneled
wishes for the strength and energy Tori needed to
face the day, along with resilience, patience, and
hope for the future.

Placing a few slices of banana on top of the shake
and sprinkling a bit of cinnamon over them, Angie
snapped on the cover and set it in front of Tori.
"Here you go."

"Thanks so much." Tori pushed a straw through
the hole in the cover and sipped. A smile spread over
her lips. "Perfect."

When she took out her wallet, Angie waved her
off and handed the woman a brown paper bag with
the Sweet Dreams Bakery logo on it. "It's on the
house today, and here are some muffins and cookies
to take with you."

A few tears gathered in Tori's eyes. "I appreciate
it, Angie." She slipped off the stool and gathered her
things.

"See you tomorrow," Angie told her with a smile.

When the bake shop closed for the afternoon, Angie locked up and went into the Victorian through the door that separated her shop from the rest of the house. She planned on changing into her running clothes and taking Gigi in the jogging stroller down to the Sweet Cove Resort on Robin's Point. Josh had owned the beautiful hotel and inn overlooking the ocean with his older brother, but Josh had bought him out and now he and Angie were the sole owners. They had a small two-bedroom bungalow on the property they could use when work kept Josh late at the resort.

When Angie walked past the dining room on the way to the staircase, she saw Courtney sitting with a woman at the long table. Courtney waved her over.

Euclid and Circe were resting on top of the dining hutch.

"This is my sister, Angie," Courtney told the woman.

"I'm Rebecca Wallace, Rachel Princeton's sister." Rebecca looked to be in her mid-thirties and had dark brown eyes and chin-length brown hair. Her eyelids were red from the tears she'd shed.

"Why don't you join us?" Courtney asked Angie.

Angie took a seat. "I'm sorry about Rachel. We've heard such good things about her."

"Thank you." Rebecca held tight to her cup of coffee. A platter of cookies, fresh fruit, and home-made granola bars were on the table and the woman had a dessert plate with some fruit on it.

Courtney said to Angie, "Rebecca only arrived a few minutes ago. She's all checked in. Ellie moved some guests around and gave Rebecca one of the carriage house apartments for her stay. More privacy that way."

Angie nodded. She noticed Violet shimmering in the corner watching them.

"Rebecca's been telling me about Rachel. She's very successful and prominent in her field," Courtney told her sister.

"I recently heard that. She's a very impressive young woman."

Rebecca said, "Rachel got the brains and the drive. I got the big bones and the good hair."

Angie raised an eyebrow at the comment. "Are you an architect, too?"

"I'm a high school math teacher. I also teach some math classes at the community college."

"Our friend and adopted family member taught math years ago," Angie said. "He's a very smart man."

Rebecca took a sip of her coffee. "I spoke with

Chief Martin at the police station before I came here. There isn't much news about my sister. He couldn't tell me much."

"It's early in the investigation," Angie said with encouragement. "The chief is an experienced and well-respected man. He's had a great deal of success in solving cases over the years. He's a good man to have on your sister's case."

"Are you and Rebecca close?" Courtney asked.

"I wouldn't say we're that close. We care about each other. We never hung out much. I'm five years older. I was in college when Rachel started high school. We didn't have much in common. We've always been in different places in our lives."

"Do you speak much?"

"Not really. I regret that. I guess as the older sister, I should be the one who reaches out, but I'm always so busy and I let that slide." Rebecca stared at her plate.

"Are your parents alive?" Courtney questioned.

"Thankfully, they aren't. This would have killed them. They were older when they had us. It's just me and Rachel. We have some cousins in New Hampshire and Vermont, but we're not close with them."

"Does Rachel have a boyfriend or a partner?" Angie asked the woman.

"She's been dating someone, but I don't think it's serious."

"What about her neighbors? Does Rachel know her neighbors?"

Rebecca's head snapped up. "I know she's familiar with one of them. He's a real jerk."

7

"Who do you mean?" Angie asked as a shiver of unease ran over her skin. "Who's a jerk?"

Rebecca screwed up her face. "Rachel's neighbor, Bob Mills. He's always causing trouble. He disputed the boundary between his place and hers and used his tractor to start ripping out the bushes growing behind their houses. Rachel got a lawyer to force him to stop destroying her property. It went to court. Guess who was right? Rachel, that's who. The jerk of a neighbor had to pay restitution costs to replace the bushes, trees, and grasses he tore out."

"Why did he do it?" Courtney asked. "Was he honestly mistaken or was there bad blood between him and Rachel?"

"You'll have to ask him, or maybe his psychologist. If he doesn't have one, he should. It made no sense at all." Rebecca picked at her cut-up fruit.

"Has there been other trouble between your sister and the neighbor?"

"Minor things," Rebecca said. "He used to complain about Rachel's dog coming onto his property. That dog never went over there. She always stayed in her own yard."

Angie glanced over to Violet.

Rebecca went on. "He used to complain that Rachel was playing loud music. She never did that."

"This has been going on for two whole years?" Courtney asked.

"It was really just the first year. I'm not sure if he bothers Rachel anymore."

"Has Rachel been trying to ignore the neighbor?" Angie questioned. "Is that why your sister hasn't mentioned anything recent?"

Rebecca shifted in her chair and then sighed. "Rachel and I had a falling out about six months ago. I haven't talked to her since then." The woman's eyes filled with tears and she cleared her throat. "I held a grudge against my sister. It was a stupid thing to do. I'm ashamed."

Courtney asked gently, "What happened between you two that caused the falling out?"

Rebecca swallowed hard. "It was right after our mother died. Our dad died of a sudden heart attack about five years ago. A year ago, our mom's health started fading. It wasn't any one thing. Things started to snowball and she went downhill fast. After she died and the will was read, I discovered my parents had left more money to Rachel than to me. Mom also left most of her jewelry to Rachel. That hurt me. My parents always seemed to favor my sister, but my Mom said she wasn't favoring anyone. She worried that Rachel didn't have a husband. I've been married for ten years. My parents thought I was set financially because we have two incomes. Rachel only has one."

Rebecca looked off across the room. "Rachel wanted to split the inheritance half and half and she wanted to give me half the jewelry." The woman sighed. "I wasn't very nice to her. I shouldn't have targeted Rachel with my anger and hurt. It was my parents' fault, not Rachel's."

A few bed and breakfast guests came into the dining room for the afternoon snacks and drinks, and when Rebecca saw them, she finished her coffee and stood. "It was nice to meet you both. I'm feeling exhausted. I'm going to head to the carriage house to shower and take a nap. I'll see you later." She took her plate and cup to the dirty dishes bin under the side table, nodded to the other guests, and left the room.

"Well," Courtney leaned close to her sister. "We got a ton of information from her. We've got a couple of people to add to the suspect list."

"Don't you mean one suspect?" Angie asked. "Rachel's neighbor."

"Yeah, him definitely." Courtney looked over her shoulder to be sure the other guests weren't listening. "And Rebecca. She hasn't talked to Rachel in over six months. All because of their parent's will. That sure is motivation to attack someone. Maybe kill someone."

"But why now?" Angie questioned. "The will was settled months ago. Why try to hurt Rachel now?"

"Maybe it wasn't settled until recently. Or maybe, something else came up regarding their inheritance. Rebecca was already upset that her sister got more than she did. Something else might have come up, and that was the last straw."

Angie looked over to the corner of the room, but Violet was no longer sitting there. "Violet was here while we talked to Rebecca."

"Did she look like she believed what the woman was saying? Did she seem hostile to Rebecca?"

"She listened with mild interest," Angie said. "I wouldn't have thought Violet knew Rebecca."

"Maybe she didn't know her. At least, she didn't show any hostility to her."

A couple of older women greeted the sisters and joined them at the table.

"Hello. You're two of the Roseland sisters, aren't you?" The woman introduced herself as Isobel Painter. Her friend was Molly Sutters.

"Yes, we are. I'm Courtney. I run the candy store on Main Street."

"I'm Angie. I own the Sweet Dreams Bake Shop."

"Oh, you have a satellite bake shop down at the museum," Molly said to Angie. "We were there today. What a lovely collection they have. And we tried some pie and coffee at the bake shop. Simply delicious."

Isobel said, "We haven't been to Main Street yet. We'll be sure to stop in at the candy store."

After a few minutes of chit chat, Isobel said, "There was some unfortunate news in town today. We heard that a resident, a young woman, is missing. Very sad. I hope the police are able to find her soon."

Angie nodded. "We hope so, too. We didn't know the missing woman. Sweet Cove is a small town, but with so many tourists coming and going all the time, it can feel a lot bigger than it is."

"Something similar happened in our town not long ago," Molly told them. "A woman went missing after her car went off the road. She was found murdered. The killer was the person you'd expect the least. Everyone was shocked."

An icy feeling enveloped Angie, and she was rubbing her arms when the doorbell rang.

Courtney went to answer it and when she opened the door, she saw Chief Martin standing on the porch.

"Got a few minutes?" he asked.

"We sure do. Come on in."

Angie hurried over when she saw the man. "Some news?" she asked quietly.

"A little."

"Let's go sit in the family room. But first, help yourself to the afternoon snacks." When the chief had poured coffee and selected a couple of cookies, Angie led the way down the hall to the back of the house.

The cats had jumped off the hutch and raced ahead them, and were sitting on the sofa when the chief, Angie, and Courtney entered the room.

"You beat us." Chief Martin scratched both of the cats' cheeks before taking a seat.

Angie and Courtney sat opposite in two comfortable chairs.

"What have you learned?" Angie was eager to hear the news.

The chief set down his coffee mug. "Rachel's laptop and desktop computer were taken from the house and examined for any clues or evidence. She had been doing some interesting internet searches."

Courtney's eyes narrowed. "Interesting how?"

"Rachel was looking up information on how to make yourself disappear," Chief Martin told them.

"Disappear? You mean like take off and no one will ever find you?" Angie asked.

"That's exactly it."

The three stared at one another for several seconds.

"She wanted to run away?" Courtney shook her head. "I don't believe it. So what was the blood from? She cut herself and smeared it around the kitchen to make it seem like someone had come in and attacked her?"

"Possibly," the chief nodded.

"That's nuts. Why would she want to run away?" Courtney's forehead was creased with disbelief.

"Rachel was well-known in her field. She was successful. Why would she throw all of that away?"

Angie sighed. "Because whatever she was afraid of was worse than losing her identity."

"That's how it looks," the chief agreed. "But we don't know for sure if Rachel followed up on the information she gathered."

"Someone might have caught up with her before she could set a plan in motion," Courtney speculated.

"That could be." The chief took a bite of a cookie. "So we add another detail to the case notes. Rachel was reading information about how to disappear. And from that, we frame some questions. Was Rachel interested in the subject for a reason other than wanting to run away herself? Did she have a compelling reason to leave her identity behind? Did the person she feared catch up to her before she could make her escape?"

"More questions and not enough answers," Angie said.

"The case is becoming stranger each day," the chief admitted. "Did she stage the attack to throw us off her trail?"

"Was she in trouble over something?" Courtney asked. "Did she have something to run from?"

"We're looking into all that."

"She's still missing, right?" Angie looked at the chief. "Are there any new clues or hints to where she might be?"

"None. Dead ends. We're talking to people who knew her ... people at work, the guy she was dating, the neighbor, friends. So far, nothing. We're looking to see if there were any disgruntled clients. Has the sister arrived?"

"She has. We spoke with her right before you got here," Courtney shared. She and Angie took turns relaying what they'd found out.

"That neighbor we talked to claimed he liked Rachel and that all the trouble they'd had was only a misunderstanding," the chief told them.

"Right." Courtney's tone was distrustful.

"The inheritance information is interesting," Chief Martin said. "We'll keep that in mind. Good work."

"What's the next step?" Angie asked.

"If any of you have the time, I'm speaking again with the neighbor. It wouldn't hurt if some of you could come along." He told them the time and both sisters agreed to go.

"I'll ask Mr. Finch if he'd like to join us," Angie said.

"Okay, good. I'd better get going. Thanks for the coffee and cookies. I'll see you tomorrow."

They walked the chief to the door and as he stepped out, Rufus came in.

He hugged Courtney and then looked over to the staircase.

"There's that odd light again." Rufus glanced all around the foyer and into the living room and dining room trying to determine the source of the light. "What *is* that?"

Angie and Courtney shared a look, and after taking a deep breath, Courtney said to her boyfriend, "I've been meaning to tell you something. Want to go for a walk?"

Alarm washed over Rufus's face. "You're not dumping me, are you?"

With a smile, Courtney took his hand. "Never. But after you hear this, I wouldn't be surprised if you dump me."

As they left the house, Angie mouthed to her sister, *Good luck*.

8

It was well after dinner and everyone was nervously waiting for Courtney to return from her walk with Rufus.

"They've been gone for hours." Jenna sat at the counter next to Libby in her highchair. "Is that a good sign or a bad one?"

"Well, there's a lot to talk about," Josh said. "So it might be a good thing."

Euclid trilled from on top of the refrigerator. Violet and Circe sat on chairs at the kitchen table across from Mr. Finch

Finch turned the page of the newspaper he was reading. "Rufus is an intelligent man. I believe he'll be open to new ideas and possibilities."

Angie stood at the kitchen island mixing ingredients in a bowl. She decided to bake to blow off her nervous energy. In her highchair, Gigi played with her small dog and cat figurines.

Ellie was making homemade pretzels and mac and cheese cups for the B and B guests. "I think Rufus is the type of person who would be open and accepting to the idea of special skills."

"You mean, like you are?" Jenna kidded her sister and everyone chuckled since Ellie herself wasn't particularly open to the idea of paranormal phenomena.

Ellie ignored the comment.

"Should I text her?" Tom asked.

Everyone in the kitchen replied in unison, "No."

"Don't interrupt them," Jenna said. "The conversation could be at a critical point and the text might stop the discussion."

"But Courtney always keeps her phone on silent," Tom protested. "What if Rufus stormed away and she's sitting somewhere alone and upset?"

Angie smiled at Tom's concern. "She knows where we are. If she needs time alone, then we shouldn't bother her."

"Anyway, they've only been gone for about five hours," Josh joked and the group laughed again.

"We need to keep talking," Angie suggested.

"The silly comments are breaking the tension we're all feeling."

"I wish they'd get back so we could stop worrying." After Ellie formed the dough into pretzel shapes and placed them into the gently boiling water, she slipped the mac and cheese muffin tins into the oven.

As if on cue, the backdoor opened and Courtney walked into the kitchen ... with Rufus right behind her. All eyes shot to their faces.

"It's okay," Rufus grinned. "I still love all of you."

Whoops of joy went up and everyone broke into applause before rushing over to the Englishman to hug him and shake his hand.

"Sorry you were the last to know," Angie told him.

"Well, to be accurate," Finch said, "our Rufus is the second to last to know. I haven't told Miss Betty yet."

"Oh, right." Jenna put her arm on Finch's shoulder. "You might want to do that one of these days."

"I'm afraid I must." Finch leaned on his cane. "But I will think of many excuses to avoid the topic before I do."

"It wasn't so bad, Mr. Finch." Rufus smiled at the man. "It was sort of like listening to Courtney tell the plot of some movie." He turned to Ellie. "Hey, Ellie, how about a demonstration of telekinesis?"

"How about not," she replied.

Rufus spotted Violet's light sparkling in the kitchen chair. "There's the dog." He walked closer and patted Circe, then looked at the glittering light. "Hello, little dog. It's nice to meet you."

"Her tail is wagging," Jenna told him. "If you try to touch the light, you can pat her. You won't feel her, but she'll feel you."

Rufus gingerly extended his hand and attempted to pat the ghost.

"She likes it," Jenna said.

Rufus chuckled with delight when the dog's particles glowed brighter. "This is amazing. You're all amazing. Except for Josh and Tom, that is."

"We can see the dog, too." Tom defended himself and his brother-in-law.

"I'm hoping the longer I hang out with Angie, the more chance I'll have to develop skills of my own," Josh said.

"That would be brilliant." Rufus looked at Courtney. "Maybe I'll develop skills. Can you teach me?"

"I'm trying to improve my own skills. Mr. Finch might be able to help you though," Courtney suggested. "He's been working with me on my abilities."

Rufus turned toward Finch. "Mr. Finch? Is there a possibility I could learn?"

Finch smiled. "I believe every person has the capability to expand and build on their senses. We can certainly try."

"If you're going to teach Rufus, then Josh and I want to be included," Tom said. "Right, Josh?"

Josh agreed. "And don't forget Jack. He'll want to be involved, too."

"We'll have a group class," Finch nodded.

Courtney leaned closer to her sisters and whispered, "This ought to be good."

"It would be cool to be a warlock." Rufus had a wide smile on his face.

"We're not witches," Angie protested.

"Yes, you are." Rufus was serious.

"It depends on the day," Tom kidded.

Courtney headed for the freezer. "This calls for ice cream. Who's with me?"

Euclid and Circe trilled while Courtney filled the bowls, and Jenna took out sprinkles, chopped nuts, and mini chocolate chips for toppings.

Angie got cream from the refrigerator and beat it into peaks of whipped cream.

The men made coffee and brought out mugs, spoons, and napkins and set the kitchen table.

"I love this family." Rufus beamed.

The next afternoon, Courtney, Angie, Mr. Finch, and Violet met Chief Martin at Rachel's house. Angie didn't want to go back inside, but she steeled herself and took a deep breath when the chief opened the door for them.

"Officers check the house a few times a day to see if Rachel made her way back home," Chief Martin told them. "So far, nothing."

When they were there last, the house had been filled with crime scene investigators and all the lights were on. In contrast to that night, the atmosphere inside was now calm and quiet, but it was an eerie quiet because they all knew what had gone on. Either someone attacked Rachel and took her away, or Rachel staged the fight and slipped away by herself.

"It feels so different here," Courtney said. She looked around the kitchen, getting a better feel for the space. Blood was still on the wall, but it wasn't as shocking as it was before. Instead of horror and revulsion, the strongest emotion they all felt was a deep, deep sadness.

"What happened?" Courtney asked no one in particular. "Was Rachel attacked and killed? Or did she escape from the person she feared would harm her?"

When Angie noticed Violet curled up on the dog bed that Rachel still kept in the corner, her heart sank into her stomach.

Mr. Finch walked around the rooms running his hand along the counters, the wall, the furniture. The others moved through the rooms trying to pick up on the energy that had been left behind the day Rachel disappeared.

When they congregated back in the kitchen, Angie shook her head. "I don't feel just one person in the house. I don't feel someone planning an escape. I sense raw fear. If I had to decide, I'd say Rachel was attacked."

"I feel the same things," Finch said. "More than one person was here. I feel their energy floating on the air, the energy they left behind that day. Fear, anger, pain."

"I agree with both of you," Courtney said. "I pick up on terrible fear, but I also feel seething rage. Two people were in this kitchen that day. Rachel wasn't alone in this room."

Chief Martin looked at them. "Okay, then. Rachel may have been thinking about taking off, but she either changed her mind or she didn't get away fast enough. Someone attacked her and probably took her away."

Everyone nodded.

"Here's the important detail ... she knew someone wanted to harm her. She knew she was in danger. That's the angle we have to investigate."

Angie thought of something. "Did Rachel clean out her bank accounts?"

"She'd recently made large withdrawals, but there was still plenty of money in the accounts."

"Were the large withdrawals unusual for her or did she do that on a regular basis?" Courtney questioned.

"It was unusual activity," the chief said.

"Then she must have been making preparations to leave." Finch placed both hands on the top of his cane.

Chief Martin looked at his watch. "We don't have to meet the neighbor for thirty minutes. Anything else you'd like to look at?"

Angie watched as Violet stood up suddenly and

trotted into the living room. She followed and saw Violet standing next to the sliding glass patio doors.

"What is it?" She walked over to see what caught the dog's attention, and when she spotted it, her breath caught in her throat. "Chief Martin," she called.

The chief, Courtney, and Finch entered the room.

"What is it, Angie?" The chief went to stand next to the young woman.

"Over there. There's a man in the bushes over by the garage."

The chief instinctively placed his hand near his weapon. "I'll go see what's going on. Stay here."

In a moment, the Roseland sisters and Finch saw the chief approach the man. Courtney slid the door open a little so they could hear what was being said.

"Mr. Mills?" the chief asked, his voice stern.

"Oh, Chief Martin." The man who emerged from the bushes was about fifty years old, had graying hair and a strong, stocky build. He was wearing jeans and a flannel shirt.

"What are you doing?" the chief asked.

"Just making sure everything's okay with Rachel's place. I cut through the bushes from my yard." Mills gestured to the tree line. "I didn't know you were stopping here before you came to my house."

"You shouldn't be doing this," the chief informed the man. "The house is a crime scene. You don't have permission to be on the property."

"Well, I was just trying to be helpful."

"If you're free, we'll come over and talk to you now. That sound all right?"

"Sure, sure. I'll see you in a few minutes." Mills plodded back through the bushes to return to his yard.

Angie made eye contact with the ghost dog and Violet whined.

Courtney rolled her eyes. "Pretty weird."

"Indeed," Finch agreed.

9

Bob Mills owned a four-acre parcel of land with a two-story house of eight rooms. A covered porch on one side of the house faced a four-car garage and a couple of other out buildings where he stored yard equipment and other tools.

Chief Martin introduced the two Roseland sisters and Mr. Finch as consultants who advised the police department.

Mills nodded his head. "Consultants, huh? You need three of them?"

The chief said, "There are two others, but they couldn't join us today."

"Must cost you a pretty penny. But I guess it's taxpayers' money anyway, so what the heck."

Angie could tell her sister was bristling at the man's words.

Courtney said, "The chief tells us you were on Rachel's property just now. Do you do that often? Go over to her place and walk around?"

"I go over to make sure everything's okay. The house is empty and its set back from the road. It's an easy target for thieves and vandals. I thought I should help out."

"That's nice of you, Mr. Mills," Finch told the man. "But I believe that the police are monitoring Miss Princeton's home."

"Yeah, the chief told me." Mills shrugged. "Just being a good neighbor. Why don't we sit on the porch? It's a nice day."

Angie watched Violet head off toward the man's garages and out buildings.

"The chief tells us that you and Rachel had a dispute about the property line," Angie started the conversation.

"Yeah." Mills shook his head. "It makes me look like a bully, but I thought that section of land was on my side of the line. I was wrong. What can I say? Everyone makes mistakes."

"You had other issues with Rachel?"

"Like what? What do you mean?"

"Something about her dog?" Angie asked.

"Oh, that. I don't want other people's animals coming over to my property. Her dog wandered over a lot at first. I asked her to keep the dog on her own land. No big deal. I have a right to do that. It doesn't make me a monster."

"No, it doesn't. We're only trying to understand the nature of the relationship."

"We didn't have no relationship. We were neighbors."

"Were? Don't you mean *are*?" Courtney asked. "Rachel is missing. She hasn't been found yet."

"Well, she's been missing for a few days now," Mills said. "I watch TV. I know the longer someone is missing, the less chance they're alive. She's been gone about three or four days now, hasn't she? That's not good. I don't think she's still alive. The odds are against it."

"Mr. Mills," Finch said, "did you hear anything on the day Rachel went missing?"

"Like what?"

"Shouting, yelling, things breaking, things falling over, angry voices. Anything like that? Anything out of the ordinary? Something you hadn't heard before coming from Rachel's house."

"I don't think so. I don't remember anything like that."

"What were you doing that day?" Angie asked.

"Same as I do every day. Work around the yard. Work on broken tools. Fix things. Work in the garden. Paint."

"What do you do for work?"

"I was a painter. I only work part-time now. I saved up. I paid off my place. I got no debt. I only take jobs when I want to."

Angie looked for Violet and saw her glittering in the sun over by a tool shed.

"Did you see anyone lurking around on the day Rachel went missing?" Finch asked. "Maybe someone in a truck you didn't recognize?"

"I don't know. Nothing sticks out in my mind."

"Can you see Rachel's house from your side?" Angie questioned.

"There are a lot of trees and bushes between us," Mills pointed out.

"Is there somewhere on your side where you can look into Rachel's yard?" Angie asked again. "Where do you walk through to get to her yard?"

"Right over there." Mills gestured. "By the big Maple. The bushes are a little thinner there. That's how I walk over to her place."

"Can we see?"

Mills shrugged. "Sure." He led the way.

Courtney said, "Oh, I see. You have a decent view of Rachel's garage from here."

Mills didn't say anything.

"Did you see anyone parked near the garage that day?" Finch brought up the question a second time.

"No. I didn't. I must have been working in the garden. It's on the other side of the house."

They started to walk back to the porch when Angie noticed Violet staring at her. She walked toward the out building.

"Where are you going?" Mills asked.

"I'd like to look around."

"Why?"

"To get a sense of how your two properties intersect." Angie was babbling anything she could think of. She felt that Violet wanted her to come to the out building.

"They don't intersect," Mills said. "They abut. We're abutters."

"What did you say you keep in the out buildings?" Angie asked.

"Tools and stuff."

The door of the shed was open and Violet went inside. Angie's heart pounded as she got closer.

"Can you show us your garden?" Finch attempted to deflect Mills's attention from Angie.

"Yeah, sure, I guess. It's this way."

Violet came back to the door from inside the shed. She pushed something along the floor with her nose.

Angie bent to pick it up. It was a small wallet. She unsnapped it and pulled out a credit card, and her vision swam for a few seconds. The name on it was Rachel Princeton.

"Angie?" the chief called to her.

When she turned to him and held up the wallet, he hurried over to her.

Mills almost jogged across the grass to the shed. "What are you doing?"

"I saw this on the floor of the shed near the doorway. I thought it was yours. I thought you must have dropped it," Angie told the man.

"It is mine." Mills tried to grab it out of her hand.

Angie shook her head and handed the wallet to Chief Martin. "It's Rachel's. Her credit cards are inside."

Courtney's eyes went wide.

Chief Martin pinned his steely eyes onto the man. "I'd like you to come down to the station for questioning."

"I found that in the bushes. I didn't do anything to Rachel." Mills's tone was a mix of defiance and fear. "I was gonna give it to you after we talked."

"I'm not accusing you of anything, Mr. Mills," the chief explained. "But the discovery of the credit card holder could be important to the case. I'd appreciate it if you would cooperate and come down to the station for an interview."

Mills exhaled loudly. "I want to tell my lawyer what's going on."

"You can certainly do that," the chief said.

Mills moved away from them, pulled his phone from his pocket, and placed a call.

While Mills was busy, the chief talked with his consultants.

"I have to take Mills back to the station to get to the bottom of this. I'll probably call a team here to go through his house. I made an appointment with the man Rachel was seeing. I told him that several consultants would be coming with me. Would you go talk to him? He's supposed to meet us at the coffee shop in Silver Cove's center."

"We can do that," Angie told him.

"How did you spot the credit card holder?" The chief kept his voice down.

"I saw Violet over here. She gave me a look. I

knew she wanted me to come to the shed. She was pushing the holder with her nose."

"It's an important find. Where is she?"

"Right here beside me." Angie touched her leg to indicate which side Violet was on.

"Good work, Violet," the chief said softly.

The dog's tail thumped the ground.

Chief Martin told the Roselands and Finch about who they were going to meet. "His name is Jason Field. He was dating Rachel. He said it was casual. I told him we wanted to ask some follow-up questions. See what you think of him. Will Violet go with you?"

"Yes," Angie said. "No one can see her except us."

"Okay, good. I'll let you know what happens with Mills. Thanks for everything." The chief waited for Mills to get off the phone.

Angie, Courtney, Mr. Finch, and Violet got into their car and headed for Silver Cove center.

"That was unexpected," Courtney said shaking her head. "Did Mills have something to do with Rachel's disappearance?"

"My first reaction is that he did have something to do with it," Finch said, "but then I remembered that Miss Rachel was so frightened about something that she was looking for information on how to disappear. I don't think she was frightened by Mr. Mills. I think she was annoyed and angry with him, but so frightened by him that she wanted to run away? I don't think so."

"Good points, Mr. Finch," Courtney said. "So what did Mills do? Break in after Rachel was taken? That's a pretty low thing to do."

"The chief will let us know."

Angie pulled the car into a small parking lot next to the coffee shop. "Here we are. Right on time, too. Let's go find Jason Field."

When they walked around to the front of the café, a tall, slender man with sandy blond hair was standing by the front door looking slightly uneasy.

"Jason? Jason Field?" Angie asked.

The man turned to them. "Yeah, that's me."

The three people introduced themselves.

"Thanks for meeting with us. Chief Martin couldn't make it today. He had to attend an unexpected meeting. He sends his apologies," Angie told him. "Shall we go inside?"

"I didn't kill Rachel," Jason blurted.

10

Angie was taken aback by the man's statement, especially since Rachel was missing and hadn't been found dead.

"Let's get a table and then we can talk." She opened the door for Courtney, Finch, Jason Field, and Violet.

Once they'd ordered and were settled in their seats, Angie made introductions. Violet sat off to the side listening, invisible to everyone but the Roselands and Finch.

"No one is accusing you of anything," Angie pointed out. "That's not why we're here. We simply want to ask some follow-up questions."

"Okay." The man didn't seem to want to make eye contact.

"Rachel is missing," Courtney told him. "She hasn't been found yet. No one is assuming she's dead. Nothing points to such a thing."

Jason's cheeks flushed. "I only meant I didn't do anything to her. She's been gone for several days now. Even the police have to admit it doesn't look good."

"The police keep that information to themselves so we're unable to confirm or deny that's what they're thinking," Finch said kindly. "As far as we know, Miss Rachel's case is that of a missing person."

The waiter brought over the coffees and set them down.

"We understand you and Rachel were seeing each other," Angie's tone made the comment seem like a question.

"We went out some times." Jason took his jacket off and hung it over the back of his chair. "It was a casual relationship."

"How long had you been seeing each other?" Angie asked.

"About seven months or so." The young man continued to seem uncomfortable with the questioning.

"Things were going well?"

"Sure."

Jason's brief answers made Angie worry that the whole interview would be like pulling teeth. "How did you meet?"

"At a friend's house. He had a few people over. We talked, we hit it off." Jason lifted the mug to his lips.

"Did you see each other every week?" Courtney was trying to get a feel for the relationship.

"Not every week. Rachel was busy, I'm busy. We'd text a few times a week even if we didn't see each other."

"What do you do for work, Mr. Field?" Finch smiled at the man to help put him at ease.

"I'm a park ranger over at the state park. I do photography, too. Nature stuff, landscapes, animals, things like that. Some of my work has been published in magazines."

"That's very impressive," Finch praised him.

"Would you describe Rachel to us." Angie held her mug in both hands.

Jason seemed surprised by the request. "Sure. Rachel was really smart."

Angie noticed the use of the past tense again.

Jason went on. "She was an architect. She wrote a book, taught college level classes, was always in demand. She had a ton of work."

With a nod and a smile, Angie encouraged him to tell more.

"We both liked hiking, cycling, and being outdoors. We liked beer, went to breweries together." He looked at the three people around the table.

"What was her personality like?" Courtney asked.

"Rachel was friendly, but she didn't need to be the life of the party. She was easy to talk to. She was kind, thoughtful. She was also very driven in her work." Jason shrugged. "It was very important to her."

Angie asked, "Did she put work over relationships?"

"I wouldn't say that. She made time for friends. She wasn't a hermit or anything, but work was definitely a priority."

"Did Rachel have any enemies?" Finch asked the young man. "Was she having trouble with anyone?"

Jason shook his head. "She didn't mention anything to me."

"Had she seemed herself the past couple of weeks?"

"Yeah, for the most part. Like I said, we didn't see each other every day or anything." As he paused, his brow furrowed. "She did seem a little weird that last time I saw her."

"Weird how?" Courtney leaned slightly forward eager to hear the reply.

Jason shifted around. "I don't know. She seemed off, kind of worried."

"Did she say what was worrying her?"

"No, she didn't. I asked her if everything was okay, and she brushed off my concern. She said things were fine, but I got the sense they weren't. At first, I thought she was tired of me, but that wasn't it. She seemed jumpy, distracted."

"What did you do the last time you saw her?"

"I went to her house. I brought over pizza and salad. It was raining so we ate inside. She wasn't her usual talkative self. I thought she probably had a lot on her mind from work, or maybe she was tired, or not feeling great." Jason shook his head. "I didn't know what it was about."

"You didn't see each other after that evening?"

"We texted the next day, but we didn't see each other. She disappeared about four days later."

"Did she have a new client?" Courtney questioned.

"I don't know. She only talked in general terms

about the work she was doing, never about specific clients."

"Was Rachel teaching this semester?"

"She wasn't. Rachel took the semester off. She told me she had too much to do to take on a teaching role this term."

"Did anything happen at work that had her concerned?"

"I don't think so."

"What about with friends? Any trouble with any of them?" Angie asked watching the man's face as he answered.

"I think everything was fine. She went to visit an old friend not too long ago." Jason's face clouded. "Rachel did seem a little antsy when she came back."

"What do you mean? How did she seem?"

"Really distracted. I asked about the visit, but she didn't seem to want to talk about it so I dropped the subject. I wondered if Rachel and her friend had an argument or something, but I didn't press her for answers.

"Where did she go? Where did the friend live?"

"Up in New Hampshire. The person she visited was an old friend from when Rachel lived there."

"Do you know her name?" Mr. Finch asked.

"Yeah, it was Jessica ... Jessica Hanson. She lived

in the town where they grew up, in Hollis. It's not far from the Massachusetts border. It's near Nashua."

Finch wrote the information in a small notebook.

Angie asked, "Did you mention to Chief Martin that Rachel was acting distracted and jumpy when you saw her last?"

Jason ran his hand over his face. "I might not have. I just remembered it while I was talking with you."

"Did you mention Rachel's friend to the chief? Did you tell him that Rachel had visited her?"

The young man shook his head. "I didn't think it was important."

"That's okay," Angie nodded. "We'll pass the information on to the chief." She looked over to Violet. The ghost dog sat like a statue watching and listening. Violet had passed away before Jason and Rachel began seeing each other. She seemed to be sizing him up.

After another twenty minutes of discussion, they thanked Jason for his time, and the man left.

Violet came closer to the table and Angie reached down to pat the dog.

"That was an interesting detail that almost didn't come up." Because the three of them were feeling hungry, Courtney had gone to the coffee shop counter and returned with three chocolate chip squares. "Rachel acted oddly after visiting her friend in New Hampshire."

"Could Rachel have been upset about something that happened between her and her friend?" Angie speculated.

"Perhaps that was the cause of her concern." Finch took a bite of the square.

"Maybe they had an argument or a falling out," Angie thought out loud. "That could have been the reason that Rachel seemed off when Jason saw her. She probably didn't want to talk about it with him."

"Do you think Chief Martin knows about Rachel's visit to her friend?" Courtney asked. "It sounds like she went to New Hampshire not long before she went missing."

Angie took out her phone. "I'll text him about it. I'll ask if he's talked to Jessica Hanson."

The three talked about how the interview had gone pointing out how nervous the young man was throughout.

"He sure didn't seem to relax while we discussed Rachel," Courtney said. "Why is he so nervous? It isn't unusual for law enforcement to speak to someone more than once in a case like this."

Angie lowered her voice. "Did either of you pick up anything about Jason?"

"I felt his uneasiness and his anxiety in having to talk about Rachel," Finch explained. "And the way he told us immediately after we said hello to him that he didn't kill Rachel was quite odd. But it doesn't mean he's guilty of the crime."

Courtney smiled. "Whenever someone blurts out that they didn't do something, I think right away that they did do it."

Angie's phone vibrated with an incoming text. She read it and then shared with Courtney and Finch what the chief had written.

"The chief says he found out Rachel went to New Hampshire to see her friend, but it wasn't Jason Field who told him. The chief called Jessica Hanson the day after Rachel went missing. The woman was distraught when he spoke with her. She said they'd had a nice weekend together and she was sorry to see Rachel leave. Rachel's sister called Jessica with the terrible news that Rachel went missing. Chief Martin has a meeting scheduled with Jessica in New Hampshire the day after tomorrow. He invites us to go if any of us are free."

"I'm in charge of the candy shop that day," Courtney said, "and Orla can't watch Gigi and Libby that day so Mr. Finch has childcare duty while you and Jenna work."

"I'd be happy to care for the girls all day if you and Jenna want to accompany Chief Martin to New Hampshire in the afternoon," Finch said.

Angie squeezed the older man's arm. "Thanks, Mr. Finch. I don't know what we'd do without you. I'll talk to Jenna about it."

11

Josh, Angie, Jenna, Tom, Ellie, Courtney, and Mr. Finch sat in the family room eating a dinner of homemade pizza and salad. Euclid lay across Courtney's lap snoozing while Circe cuddled next to Finch. Violet was resting on the rug in front of the fireplace and Libby and Gigi were playing with toys in the playpen.

"We need a night off from the missing person case and work and everything else," Courtney announced.

"Shall we all watch a movie?" Finch asked as he reached for his napkin.

"I was thinking of something more active," she told him.

"What do you have in mind?" Josh put another piece of pizza on his plate.

"I was thinking since it's September already, we should go to the corn maze."

"Right now? Tonight?" Tom asked.

"Sure, why not? It's a beautiful night and it's not cold," Courtney tried to convince them. "And it will only get more crowded the closer we get to Halloween."

"We did it last year," Jenna noted. "It was a lot of fun."

"It will take our minds off Rachel's case and put us in the holiday spirit," Courtney said. "It's open until 11pm. We'd have plenty of time to do it."

"I think it's a fine idea," Finch grinned. "Will we break into teams again like last year?"

"A little friendly competition wouldn't hurt," Josh agreed.

"I'm going to call Jack and ask him to come," Ellie reached for her phone.

"Rufus is coming here in about fifteen minutes," Courtney said. "I ran the idea past him earlier today and he's onboard."

"Miss Betty is in a training class this evening," Finch said. "So without her the sides will be uneven. Oh, but the girls. I can stay home and watch them."

"No, no, Mr. Finch, you need to come," Courtney told them. "I talked to two of our candy shop employees today and they said they'd be glad to watch Libby and Gigi. One will stay here and the other one will go to Jenna and Tom's house. By the time we leave, the kids will be in bed anyway. It will be easy babysitting duty."

"But the sides will be uneven," Finch protested.

"I thought about that," Courtney said. "The teams will be the women against the men so it's okay if you have one more team member than we do. You'll need him," she kidded.

"Jack's on his way," Ellie announced.

"Okay, it's settled. I'll call the babysitters and tell them what time to report for duty." Courtney stood. "I'll handle the dishes and cleanup while you all get ready."

When they arrived at the corn maze, the lot was nearly full, but they were able to find places to park their two cars.

The half-moon shone bright overhead in a sky full of stars.

"Can you believe how many people are here?" Jenna looked around in amazement.

The group bought tickets to the maze, but they had an hour before their entry time so they wandered around. A bonfire blazed off to one side, a band played on the stage, food trucks lined up along a field selling everything from tacos, wings, barbecue, soft serve ice cream, burgers, and corn dogs. A beer garden was on another side of the field with long tables set under strings of tiny white lights. There was an enormous pyramid made of hay bales that could be climbed on, a huge trampoline, and lots of games like corn hole, badminton, and croquet.

"This is great," Josh looked around. "It's even better than last year."

"We don't even need to do the maze," Tom said. "We can have a fun night wandering around out here."

Everyone got a cup of warm cider, Courtney bought some cotton candy, Angie and Jenna purchased containers of popcorn to share with the others, and Mr. Finch got a candy apple. Even though they'd all had dinner, Jack, Tom, Rufus, and Josh ate chicken wings and hot dogs.

Ellie and Jack walked hand in hand in front of

the group, talking and gazing into one another's eyes.

"When are those two going to get engaged?" Courtney asked. "They've been making goo-goo eyes at each other for the past two years."

Angie looked at her youngest sister. "We could ask the same of you and Rufus."

"We're too young, but Ellie and Jack aren't getting any younger," Courtney responded.

Finch chuckled. "I'm sure Miss Ellie and Jack would love to hear that."

"And what about you, Mr. Finch?" Courtney asked. "Betty's been mooning over you for quite a while. Are you going to ask her to marry you one of these days?"

"I think Miss Betty and I are happy the way things are." Finch held his cane in one hand and his candy apple in the other.

"Really? You aren't going to tie the knot some-day?" Jenna asked.

"Not unless we decide to have children," Finch joked, making the sisters laugh.

"We like having you live in the Victorian with us," Angie told him. "It wouldn't be the same if you moved into Betty's house."

"I like the way things are," Finch told them. "In all my life, I have never been happier."

Courtney leaned over and kissed the man on the cheek. "If Rufus and I do get married, I want you to walk me down the aisle."

"It would be an honor to do so," Finch beamed.

"Our time for the maze is coming up," Josh announced after he, Tom, and Rufus returned from climbing the pyramid. "We should go over to the entrance."

The group moved through the field to wait until their time was called.

"Come on, guys," Tom roused the men. "We need to put our game faces on."

"Right," Rufus said. "We can't let the women beat us again this year."

"Ellie, come on over here with us," Jenna called to her sister. "Try to tear yourself away from Jack for the next hour. No fraternizing with the enemy."

Jack placed a sweet kiss on Ellie's lips and they separated to join their teams.

"You can blow him kisses from over here," Courtney teased.

Ellie smiled at her sisters and playfully told them, "You can make fun of us all you want. Our love for one another is a shield that will defend us from your silly comments."

Angie, Jenna, and Courtney broke out in laughter.

"Next group," the ticket taker called. "Come forward."

When they stepped forward, a sudden rush of dread and doom washed over Angie like a cold ocean wave, but in a moment, it faded away as she listened to Courtney whisper their game plan so the men couldn't hear it.

The ticket taker went over the rules of the maze and wished them a fun time. "There are workers throughout the maze wearing yellow vests. If you can't find your way out, just ask one of them for help and they'll be happy to assist you. Okay, ready, set, go."

The family and friends darted into the maze with one team heading in one direction and the other team rushing the opposite way.

There were three elevated wooden bridges in the maze where maze-goers could go up and get an over-view of where they were in relation to the exit. It often didn't help at all, but once in a while, it gave a puzzler a clue.

The women stood atop one of the bridges and

could see the men walking along the path down below. The teams trash-talked and jeered good-naturedly at each other before continuing on their ways.

Back down in the maze, the women got confused and ended up going in the same circle three times when Ellie suddenly had a revelation. She pointed out that they'd missed a turn they were looking for, thinking it was on the left side when it was really on the right. They quickly headed off again, found the turn they wanted, and hurried down the new pathway. In less than five minutes, they spotted the exit and began to jog.

Coming from the opposite pathway, they heard Jack yell, "Here it is. This is the way out."

With Ellie in the lead, Courtney, Angie and Jenna sprinted the final yards and emerged from the maze just before the men.

With joyful whoops, they celebrated their win, and then applauded and clapped the men on their backs as they completed the labyrinth.

"We were so close," Tom said.

"I thought we had them this time," Jack agreed.

"It was nearly a tie this year," Ellie said. "We all did a great job."

"And we all finished ten minutes faster than last year, too," Courtney smiled.

"Success all around," Mr. Finch told them. "It was truly energizing."

As they headed for their cars, Angie suggested, "Let's all meet at the Victorian. We can have some hot cocoa before we say goodnight."

Back at the house, the cats and Violet greeted the family and friends and everyone went to the kitchen to make the cocoa and rehash the successes and errors made while in the maze.

"Next year," Rufus said, "I think we should get to one of those bridges early on to get an overview of things. Then we can make a plan and go from there."

"It's worth a try," Jack nodded. "That could be a good strategy."

The hot cocoa was poured into mugs, whipped cream was placed on top, and they all gathered around the kitchen island chatting and sipping the chocolatey sweet liquid.

When the doorbell rang, they all stared at each other.

"One of the B and B guests must have forgotten the door code," Ellie said.

"I'll go let them in." Angie headed out of the kitchen, down the hall, and into the foyer.

Violet stood near the front door looking forlorn.

Oh, no, Angie thought as a rush of adrenaline raced through her veins.

She opened the door to see Chief Martin standing under the porch light.

"I'm sorry to come so late," the man said, "but I wanted to tell you all in person. Rachel Princeton's body was found a little while ago. She's dead."

12

The chief joined everyone in the kitchen and repeated the sad news he'd told Angie in the foyer. Euclid hissed and Circe let out a long mournful howl.

No one said a word for several seconds as the reality of the announcement hit them.

"I am very sorry to hear this news," Mr. Finch said with a solemn tone. "I wish the young woman a peaceful passage to the other side."

"Where was she found?" Courtney's voice was hoarse when she spoke.

"In the woods about a quarter mile from the farm and corn maze."

Angie remembered the feeling of dread that had

come over her while waiting to enter the maze and knew it must have been from sensing Rachel nearby.

"How did she die?" Ellie asked the question that was on everyone's mind.

"From stab wounds. It seems she bled out. We won't know until the coroner completes his report if Rachel died in the woods or died elsewhere and was dumped," the chief told them.

Violet stood in the corner, her particles alternating between fading to almost nothing to becoming so bright it was hard to look at her.

Angie went over to the dog and bent down to hold her. "I'm so sorry about Rachel, Violet. I know it won't bring her back, but we'll find out who did this .... and that person will spend the rest of his life in prison."

"What about the neighbor who had Rachel's credit card holder?" Jenna asked the chief. "Was there anything to hold him on? Could he be the one who did this?"

"His story seems to hold water," The chief reported. "He claims to have found it in the area of trees and bushes between his property and Rachel's. It was found near her garage."

"That's where the cats spotted the truck tire print," Angie pointed out.

Chief Martin nodded. "We don't know whose truck made the print. We don't know if Rachel had an appointment with a repair person, if someone she knew stopped by, or if it was some kind of delivery. No one reports seeing a truck going down her driveway. For now, it's a dead end. And there's nothing we can charge the neighbor with."

"Was the murder weapon recovered?" Jack asked.

"No, it hasn't been, but there is a kitchen knife missing from the holder on the counter near the stove in Rachel's place."

"That's interesting," Angie said. "Maybe the killer came to the house without intending to murder Rachel, a fight broke out, and the attacker grabbed the knife from the holder."

"It's certainly a possibility." The chief straightened his shoulders. "It's been a long evening. I'm going home. Lucille says she can't remember who I am because she never sees me." The chief's wife was a friendly, intelligent, and loving woman who patiently understood the demands of her husband's position. "I'll pick you up tomorrow afternoon?" he asked Angie and Jenna.

"We'll be ready," the sisters told him.

∼

The next afternoon, while riding in Chief Martin's patrol car to the town of Hollis, New Hampshire, Angie, Jenna, and the chief discussed the twists and turns of the case.

"Jessica Hanson and Rachel grew up together?" Angie asked from the backseat.

"They met in kindergarten and stayed friends all these years." The chief moved the vehicle onto the highway for the forty-minute drive.

"What do you know about Jessica?" Jenna asked.

"She runs marathons, invests in real estate, owns four rental properties, flips houses. She started small, bought one house, fixed it up and sold it at a profit. She talked to me for quite a while when I spoke on the phone with her. She's personable, sounds smart. She went to college for business, always wanted to be her own boss. She loves what she does. Jessica thinks the world of Rachel, admires her drive and ambition to be one of the best in her field. She told me she and Rachel have the best time together, no matter if they're hiking, sitting in the living room watching a movie, or going out dancing with friends."

"It will be good to get her impressions about what's going on in the case," Angie said. "Jessica sounds like she has a good head on her shoulders. Does she know that Rachel has been found?"

"I called her early this morning. She didn't answer the call. I left her a message saying I had some news to share with her and to please call me back."

"Did she call?" Jenna asked.

"She did not. That tells me she must have heard about Rachel and won't return my call since we have the meeting this afternoon," the chief surmised.

"Such horrible news to hear," Jenna said. "She must be distraught."

"I was hoping she didn't cancel our meeting," the chief said.

"Did Jessica say anything about how Rachel seemed when they got together for the weekend?" Angie questioned.

"She told me Rachel seemed like her usual self. She was happy and optimistic, as always."

"Could Jessica be Rachel's killer," Angie asked. "Did something happen between them that weekend? Did Jessica go down to Sweet Cove to talk to Rachel? Did things go bad and Jessica grabbed the knife?"

"It's sure possible. We intend to pull her cell phone records," the chief said. "See if she was where she tells us she was." He moved the car into the middle lane of the highway. "We haven't talked much about Rachel's boyfriend, Jason Field. Any more thoughts about him?"

Angie said, "We don't have feelings one way or the other about him. It was strange when he blurted out he didn't kill her, but that could be put down to nervousness and concern about why we were interviewing him a second time. He had a lot of nice things to say about Rachel. The relationship didn't seem serious. Both Jason and Rachel were wrapped up in their jobs and didn't have a lot of free time to devote to building a connection. It seems they weren't yet in places where a relationship was important to them."

"Where was he the day Rachel was attacked?" Jenna asked.

"He was at the state park working," the chief said. "Some people saw him there, but no one has told us he was there at the time of the crime. Cell service isn't great there so that didn't help pinpoint where he was. It wouldn't have taken him long to drive to Rachel's house from the park ... fifteen minutes at most."

"We didn't ask him where he was since he'd already told you when you interviewed him the other day." Angie watched the scenery go by. The trees had started turning colors and the leaves were different shades of yellow, green, red, and orange. "It's hard to believe it's only been four days since this whole thing started. It feels like forever."

Chief Martin used the GPS in the car to find Jessica's house. It was a well-kept two-story place set back a little from the quiet lane with a wide front porch. A two-car garage sat to the left of the home. The landscaping was nicely-done with flowering bushes and flowers planted around the porch and several mature shade trees dotted the front lawn. A few pumpkins lined the steps to the front door.

"It's a very nice house," Jenna observed. "It's big, but looks cozy."

The chief parked and got out, then headed to the front door where he rang the bell.

"This won't be an easy interview," Angie said, "with her just learning that her friend is dead."

The chief pressed the doorbell again and they waited.

"Maybe she's out back in the yard," Jenna suggested.

They walked around the side of the house, but the woman wasn't there.

"Maybe she went somewhere after hearing about

Rachel," the chief said. "She may have completely forgotten about our meeting. I'll give her a call." Chief Martin took out his phone and placed the call. It went to voicemail.

"Why don't we knock on the backdoor," Angie said. "Maybe she didn't hear the front bell ring." She walked up the steps and pressed the bell. She heard its chime so they knew it was working.

Again, no one came to the door.

"Why don't you call her one more time," Jenna told the chief. "She may have been on another call when yours came through."

The chief tried again and while he waited for the woman to pick up, Angie leaned closer to the backdoor.

"The phone's ringing inside the house," she told them. "End the call and then try again. Let's see if it's her cell that's ringing."

As soon as the chief ended the call, the ringing stopped. When he placed it again, Angie heard it inside.

"She left her phone behind." A rush of adrenaline pulsed in her veins. "How likely is that?"

"Not very." The chief quickly mounted the steps and bent to look inside through the window. "Jessica," he yelled. "Are you inside?"

"You think she's in there?" Jenna's voice held a tone of worry.

Chief Martin banged on the window glass and called the woman's name again. "I can see her purse on the kitchen island."

"I doubt she left the house without her purse." Angie tried to peek into the kitchen window, but it was too far from her to see anything."

Jenna ran around the back and side of the house trying to see inside.

"Can we break in?" Angie asked.

"I'm out of my jurisdiction. I'm calling the local police."

The chief made the call for help, and then they waited.

13

The local police arrived and Chief Martin introduced himself and the two sisters and explained that they had arrived for a meeting with Jessica Hanson to discuss the murder of her friend in Sweet Cove.

"When Chief Martin calls Jessica's phone, we can hear it ringing inside," Angie told them. "And there's a purse on the kitchen counter."

The first officer asked the three people to stay on the patio while they investigated the house so Angie, Jenna, and the chief went down the steps to wait hoping that Jessica had mistakenly left her phone inside.

"Maybe she's out for a walk," Jenna said. "She could be trying to clear her head and lost track of the time."

"Maybe." The chief's facial muscles were tight. He didn't seem to think Jenna's theory was correct.

After the two officers repeatedly rang the bell, they decided to walk around the house trying to peer in the windows. They soon returned to the backdoor.

"We're going to break the window in the door to gain entry to the home," the first officer alerted the chief.

They used a Billy club to bash in the window, then one of them reached inside to unlock the door and the two officers disappeared into the house.

"I'm a nervous wreck." Angie moved from foot to foot.

"What's taking them so long?" Jenna asked.

One of the officers hurried out, dashed down the steps, turned to face the house, bent at the waist, and had dry heaves.

Jenna reached for her sister's arm. "Oh, no."

Angie's heart dropped and when she looked at the chief, he slowly shook his head.

The second officer charged out and hurried to the police car parked by the garage. "I have to call it in. Don't go in there."

Once the first officer recovered, he walked over to Chief Martin. His face was as white as a sheet. Shakily, he said, "The woman is dead. Once the detective arrives, he might allow you in."

Police sirens could be heard getting closer, and within minutes a swarm of officers rushed into the house.

"What the heck is going on?" Angie asked. "First Rachel, now Jessica?"

"The deaths have to be related." Jenna stared at the people moving around the yard.

An ambulance arrived, and the EMTs hurried into the house.

"It seems so, but in what way?" the chief asked. "Did the woman commit suicide over the death of her friend? Was she already suffering from depression and Rachel's murder pushed her over the edge?"

"I didn't think of that," Angie admitted.

"It could also be a terrible coincidence with two random attackers," the chief said. "Or are the deaths connected? Did they do something to anger someone? What are the links between the women and the attacker?"

Angie and Jenna continued to watch the police do their work.

"Jessica could have suffered a death from natural causes," the chief offered another possibility. "But I might discount that option since the first officer came hurrying out of the home and practically got sick. That tells me it wasn't a heart attack or even an accidental overdose. The scene is something that shocked and sickened an officer. Violence must have been inflicted, either self-inflicted or by another person. We'll have to wait to be briefed by one of the officers or a detective."

"What a mess. Can I text Courtney, Ellie, and Mr. Finch to let them know what's happened?" Jenna asked.

"Sure. Just tell them to keep it to themselves for now."

With a brisk step, an officer came over to the chief. "Detective Myers would like to speak with you, if you don't mind."

The chief nodded, told the sisters he wouldn't be long, and followed the man to a tent that had been set up near the garage.

"My guess is there's a ninety percent chance the two deaths are related." Jenna crossed her arms over her chest and continued to watch the commotion.

"Not ninety-nine percent sure?" Angie asked.

"That's probably closer to the truth."

"The chief might be with the detective for a

while. Let's sit. We're not in anyone's way over here." Angie and her sister took seats on the patio.

"Do you feel anything?" Jenna asked.

"Besides horror and disbelief, I'm not sure what I feel. I'd like to get inside that house so we can try to sense what went on, but that won't happen this afternoon."

"The door wasn't unlocked," Jenna said. "The door wasn't jimmied or smashed. So was it someone Jessica knew?"

"The police must have checked the front door when they were trying to find out if Jessica was at home. It must have been locked, too. It might not have been someone she knew. She might have thought it was Chief Martin arriving early for the meeting. And anyway, it's daytime, if someone rang at the Victorian or at your house, you'd answer the door to see who it was."

"I might not anymore," Jenna sighed.

"I know what you mean. We should get one of those camera things so you can see who's ringing the bell without opening the door to them."

"What in the world could have happened that it angered someone to the point of killing them?" Jenna asked.

"Money? Drugs? I just don't know." Angie looked

at her sister. "Something might have happened that weekend when Rachel came up here for a visit. Rachel's sometime boyfriend told us Rachel was acting a little odd when she came back from her weekend away. She was jumpy, he said. She seemed distracted. The timing is right. I wonder when Rachel started to search the internet for information about running away and disappearing. If it was before she visited Jessica, then what they did that weekend probably wasn't the thing that caused all this."

Jenna said, "But if she researched disappearing *after* the weekend with Jessica, then the time they spent together might have been the factor that caused their deaths."

"We need more information," Angie said. "We need to know what they did that weekend." She looked over at the tent where the chief was speaking with the detective. "I'd love to know what's being said."

"You and me both."

"They'll probably swear him to secrecy and he won't be able to tell us anything," Angie worried.

"We'll pull it out of him."

A wail pierced the air and Jenna and Angie whirled around to see a woman in her thirties rushing down the driveway, crying. An officer took her arm while another officer reached for the other arm, and they talked softly to her.

"A relative?" Jenna suggested.

"A sister maybe."

Chief Martin emerged from the tent and the officers ushered the crying woman inside.

The chief sat down next to the sisters. "That's Jessica's sister, Julia. That won't be an easy conversation the detective is about to have with her." He looked from Angie to Jenna. "Short story is they don't have a clue what happened here, but they're very concerned to hear that she and Rachel were long-time friends. I told them what we know so far about Rachel ... which isn't a whole lot." He paused and took in a deep breath. "Jessica's forearms were badly slashed. Initially, it might appear to be a suicide, but because of the young woman's connection to Rachel, it is suspected that an attacker cut her to make it look like she slashed her own wrists. The crime scene investigators have to do their thing and the medical examiner will report her findings. So we'll see. It will be a few days until they make their determination."

"Wow," Jenna shook her head. "What a mess."

"Will they let you inside to see the body?" Angie asked.

"If I asked, they'd let me in, but there's no need for me to do that. I'll have access to the crime scene photos and all the reports. The detective told me I can speak with Jessica's sister as soon as he briefs her. He and I will interview her together. You can sit in with us as well, but only to listen."

"Okay. We can do that." Angie nodded.

Jenna said, "There's no evidence of forced entry, right?"

"That's right. Jessica must have opened the door to whoever rang the bell. Either she knew the person, or she opened the door to see what the person wanted. I don't think she thought it was us. She's been dead for about two or three hours. We wouldn't have arrived hours early for the meeting."

Angie agreed with the chief's idea. "Did Rachel do her internet sleuthing on how to disappear before or after she visited Jessica for the weekend?"

"After."

"So that makes me think that Jessica and Rachel somehow crossed paths with their killer," Angie said.

"Or Rachel was already worried about some-thing, she discussed it with Jessica, and they came up with the idea of running away without leaving a trace," the chief said. "Jessica's devices will be searched to see whether she also looked for information on how to disappear. If she did, they'll determine when she did the searches. If it was when Rachel was here, or shortly thereafter, then Jessica may have been trying to help her friend, or they were both in danger and were planning to escape together."

"If they were that afraid, why wouldn't they go to the police?" Jenna asked.

"For some reason, they probably didn't think it would help them," the chief said.

"This thing is like a huge spider's web with the web going off in all directions," Angie said.

The chief nodded. "We just have to figure out who the spider is who's sitting in the middle of it all."

14

Angie, Jenna, and Chief Martin were invited into the tent to meet Jessica's sister, thirty-five-year old Julia Hanson-Smith. The woman sat in a metal folding chair dabbing at her wet, red eyes. Julia carried a few extra pounds and had brown chin-length hair.

Detective Myers introduced Chief Martin and the chief introduced Angie and Jenna.

"Things like this don't happen around here," Julia sniffed. "My poor sister. Who would do such a terrible thing?"

"Your sister and Rachel Princeton were friends, is that correct?" the chief started the discussion.

Julia nodded. "Since they were little. They did everything together. Now they're both gone. Do you have a suspect in Rachel's death?"

"Not yet," the chief said. "We hope to soon."

"Did the same person kill both of them?" Julia used the wadded up tissue to dab again at her eyes. "Do you think that's what happened?"

"I'm afraid it's too soon to say," Detective Myers told the woman.

"Well, what in the world happened here?" Julia demanded to know.

"The investigation has only just started," the detective explained with a gentle tone.

"Did you know that Rachel came to visit your sister for the weekend not long ago?" the chief questioned.

"Yes, I knew. I came by to see Rachel. It was really nice to see her." Julia let out a sound like a hiccup.

"How did she seem?"

"She was friendly and pleasant like she always is. She's an upbeat person. She's nice to be around." Julia bit her lower lip. "Was ... she *was* nice to be around."

"Did she talk to you about being worried about anything? About someone being angry over something?"

"No, Rachel didn't mention anything like that to me," Julia said with conviction. "She seemed happy."

"Did she talk about her work?"

"Rachel never talked in detail about her work. She might tell us what she working on, but it was explained in general terms, no specifics." Julia gripped her hands together with the tissue trapped in between.

"Was she excited about her projects?" the chief asked.

"She was very upbeat about her work."

"Did she talk about a boyfriend?"

"She'd been seeing a guy for several months. She was still with him. Rachel told us that she liked the man, but it was a casual thing. They might go a couple of weeks without seeing each other." Julia's eyes widened. "You don't think her boyfriend killed her, do you?"

"We don't have any suspects at this time," the chief said. "Did Rachel's boyfriend ever come up with her to visit Jessica?"

"No, I don't think Jessica ever met him. I certainly had not."

The chief asked quietly, "Did your sister ever think of harming herself?"

Julia sat straight. "Hurt herself? No way. You think it was suicide? Absolutely not. My sister wouldn't do such a thing. She did not die from anything self-inflicted. It's out of the question. I'm one-hundred percent sure of that. She loved her life, her work, her house."

"Did Jessica talk about anything that was bothering her?"

"No, she didn't."

"Anything said in passing, like an argument with a business associate, a contractor, a client?" the chief asked.

"Nothing out of the ordinary. When you work with people ... when you work with the public, you always have some things that don't go perfectly well. People can be difficult. Jessica could always smooth over anything that might be bothering someone. She was a people person. She listened. People liked her."

Except for one person who didn't, Angie thought to herself.

"Were there any snags in a deal she was doing?"

Julia shook her head. "She never mentioned a word about any snags or problems."

"Did she seem worried or concerned about anything?" the chief asked again.

"There are always concerns when you're working in real estate, but there was nothing out of the ordinary."

"You and your sister were close?" The detective asked the woman.

"We were very close." Julia's eyes watered, but she was able to keep the tears from falling.

"Did you talk often?"

"Almost every day." Julia closed her eyes for a few moments and then swallowed. "There will be a huge hole in my life now."

Angie watched Julia's face. There was something about what she was saying that didn't ring true. She wondered if the emotion Julia was showing was real. What she was saying and displaying didn't seem to reach the woman's eyes. Angie felt something was off.

"When did you see your sister last?" Angie asked.

Julia looked almost startled that Angie had asked a question. "Ah, um, let's see. The day I came over to see Rachel."

"That was what? About two weeks ago?"

"About that, yes."

"And if Detective Myers looks up your phone records, he'd see calls between you and Jessica almost every day?"

"Well, not *every* day." Julia looked away from Angie.

"Did you and Jessica get along?"

"Of course, we did."

"Did you hang out together? Get dinner

together? Do things outside with each other?"

Julia's face seemed to harden. "Jessica was an athlete, I'm not. Jessica was always busy with work or with working out. She didn't have a lot of time. I'd meet her for coffee once in a while. We didn't have a lot of time together."

Angie nodded. "What do you do for work?"

"I'm a nurse practitioner. It's not as lucrative as what Jessica did for work, but I like my job and I'm proud of my skills."

Angie sensed some competition between the sisters. "It's an important profession."

"It is. We do good work." Some tears began to flow. "I'm feeling very tired. Is there much more you want to talk to me about?"

The detective and the chief exchanged glances, and Detective Myers said, "I think we're all done for now, but we both might want to speak to you again. I'll share your contact information with the chief. Thank you for your time. Again, our condolences about your sister."

Julia nodded, stood, and left the tent.

"Sorry for asking a few questions," Angie told them. "What Julia was saying didn't ring true to me. They clearly didn't have the buddy-buddy relationship she was trying to portray."

"I agree. I'll look into where she was around the time Jessica was attacked. She told me she was at home. I'll find out if that was so. Thanks for your help with the interview." Detective Myers nodded at the chief. "I'll be in touch." He excused himself and left the tent.

"So Jessica didn't take her own life? That's off the table?" Jenna asked.

"I'd say so. Whoever attacked her made it look as if she might have hurt herself, but I'm not buying it," Chief Martin said.

"Neither am I," Angie agreed with him.

"Good," Jenna said, "because I don't think she killed herself either. What about the sister? Is she a suspect?"

"I'd sure put her on the list." The chief stretched his back muscles. "How about we head home?"

It was dark when the chief dropped Angie and Jenna back at their homes. Angie walked into the Victorian to find Euclid, Circe, and Violet waiting for her in the foyer.

"Hello, best cats and dog," Angie patted each one

of them. "It was a very long afternoon. Rachel's friend has been murdered."

After Euclid threw back his head and howled, they followed Angie into the kitchen where she made a cup of tea. "Where's everyone else?" she asked the animals.

They trotted into the empty family room and over to the door to Mr. Finch's apartment.

Holding her tea mug in one hand, Angie knocked on the doorframe of the open door.

"I'm here," Finch called from inside.

Walking through the kitchen-dining room and crossing the living room, Angie headed to the cozy sunroom where Finch had his easel set up.

"Miss Angie," he called to her. "Here I am." He spun on his swivel stool to face her. "How are you? What an awful afternoon you've had. It was terrible news."

The cats and the glittering dog jumped onto the small sofa.

Throughout the afternoon and early evening, Angie had sent texts to the family with information on the murder of Jessica Hanson.

Sinking into a chair, she leaned back against the soft cushion. "I sure wasn't expecting to discover Jessica dead." She filled in more details for Finch and answered his questions before asking, "Where is everyone?"

"Josh had something to tend to at the resort and he took Gigi with him. Miss Ellie is at the select-board meeting and Miss Courtney is at the candy shop. They'll be home soon. Did Jenna go home?"

Angie gave a nod. "Chief Martin dropped her off at her house."

"How are you feeling? Can I get you something? We wrapped up a plate for you from dinner. Shall I warm it up?"

Angie smiled at the kind man. "I can do it. I don't want to interrupt your painting."

"Oh, that's all right. I'd rather talk with you. Why don't we go to the big kitchen so you can eat?" Finch stood and Angie was able to better see his painting.

"That's beautiful. What a lovely scene." She walked over to admire the man's work. Finch had painted a cozy-looking farmhouse set on acres of trees and meadows with a field of pumpkins. Some of the leaves on the trees were just beginning to change colors.

"Have you seen this place?" Angie asked.

"No, I haven't. At least, not to my knowledge. It just came into my mind when I picked up my brush to start a new painting."

Something about the artwork pulled at Angie, and she stared at it letting her eyes roam over the canvas. "When did you start working on this?"

"The day after Rachel Princeton went missing." Finch covered his paint palate and collected his brushes to bring them to the kitchen sink for cleaning. "I'll just clean these off before we go to the main kitchen."

Angie remained rooted in place still looking at the new painting. An art-lover, collector, and artist, Mr. Finch sometimes mysteriously drew or painted images that held clues to a case they were working on without knowing the significance until later.

"Miss Angie?" Finch had completed the cleaning task and was standing in his living room looking into the sunroom.

The young woman startled when he called her name. "I'm coming. I was admiring your work."

The cats and dog jumped off the sofa, darted out of the apartment ahead of Finch and Angie, and raced into the Victorian's family room.

Leaning on his cane, Finch pinned his eyes on Angie. "Is there something ... *interesting* about the painting?"

"I'm not sure." Angie shrugged one of her shoulders. "Maybe?"

15

Angie sat at the kitchen island eating her dinner and Finch was heating water for tea when Courtney came into the house and hung her jacket in the back hall.

"Everything okay?" The young woman went to her sister and gave her a hug.

"I'm okay. It's been a long day."

"It must have been such a shock." Courtney sliced a piece from the apple pie on the counter and carried her plate over to sit next to her sister. "I'm glad Jenna was with you. Is she doing okay, too?"

"Yeah, she is."

Carrying her briefcase, Ellie came into the room wearing a dark green dress and a camel hair jacket. "I'm back from the meeting. It ran late." Ellie was a member of the town selectboard. "What a day you had," she said to Angie. "Can you tell me about it or do you need a break? Want to wait until tomorrow to talk about it?"

"No, I can tell you." Angie retold the story of being at Jessica's house and realizing something was amiss, calling the police, waiting around for news, and interviewing Jessica's sister, Julia. "We're putting her on the suspect list for now. She made it seem like she and Jessica were close, but there were holes in her comments and I think she was jealous of her sister. The chief will look into where she was around the time of the murder."

"Two friends murdered in two states." Ellie shook her head. "What in the world is going on?"

Finch said, "Miss Angie is interested in the painting I'm doing right now."

One of Courtney's eyebrows raised. "Oh?"

Ellie looked at her sister. "Interesting how?"

"The way you think it is," Angie told them. "I was drawn to it. I couldn't stop looking at it. There's something about it."

"It's the farmhouse scene?" Courtney asked to be sure she knew which piece of artwork was being discussed.

"It is," Finch said.

"The farmhouse in the painting isn't Rachel's place though, right?"

"It is not."

"Do you know where the farmhouse in your painting is located?" Ellie questioned.

"I don't. I thought it came from my imagination."

"Well, if Angie can't stop looking at it, I'd guess it's from more than your imagination," Courtney speculated. "It must be a clue. How can we find out where it is?"

"I think we'll have to wait and see what else presents itself in the case," Angie said.

"I really don't like waiting," Courtney said and turned to Finch, "but we'll all be on the lookout for anything that can give us more information about what's in your painting."

After a little more discussion about the painting and the murder cases, Angie asked Ellie how her meeting went.

"It was routine stuff, at least until the end."

"How do you mean?" Courtney asked.

"I've been approached to run for State Representative."

"What?!" Courtney's eyes went wide.

"Oh, my gosh, Ellie," Angie said. "That's amazing."

"How wonderful," Finch smiled broadly.

"It took me by surprise." Ellie poured herself of cup of tea. "The current state rep is retiring. A group of people are looking for a good candidate. They talked with me after the board meeting. I barely said anything, I was so dumbfounded. They asked me to think it over, give it some consideration. They think I'd have a good chance of winning."

"Well, wow," Courtney hugged Ellie. "What great news."

"I never even considered running for something like that." Ellie sipped her tea.

"You're going to do it, aren't you?" Courtney asked.

Ellie looked at them. "I don't know."

"What are you thinking?" Angie questioned. "Want to talk it over with us?"

"It's a huge compliment to be asked to run, and I think I'd really like representing the area and working to try to make things better. I'd like to do more to help people."

"I hear a *but* coming," Courtney observed.

"But would I be able to still run the B and B?"

"We could all pitch in and help with that," Angie offered.

"I'd be in Boston a lot of the time and I'd be

working here in the district talking to people, finding out about their needs." Ellie looked down at her mug. "It would be more than a full time job. And you all have full time jobs yourselves."

"We can help with the inn, but you might need to hire an assistant manager to oversee things while you're busy with state business," Finch said. "A manager would provide continuity of service and keep things running smoothly."

"That's a good idea." Angie agreed with the suggestion.

"But then *I* wouldn't be running it anymore, at least not the day to day stuff." Ellie frowned. "I like running the B and B. I enjoy meeting the guests, making the breakfasts, helping them plan their trips, making their vacations pleasant and interesting. I'd miss it."

"But would you miss it more than you'd enjoy working in government at the state level?" Courtney asked. "You would be a great state rep. You're smart, hardworking, honest, compassionate. You'd do so much for the area."

Ellie thanked her sister for the compliments. "I just don't know."

"Give it some time, Miss Ellie," Finch suggested. "Go over the pros and cons. Think about where you'd like to be in the future. What work would you like to be doing? You don't have to make a decision tonight. Talk it over with Jack, too. Get his opinion."

"I will." Ellie sighed. "Right now, I don't have a clue what to do."

"Both options are great," Angie smiled. "You can't go wrong with whatever you decide to do."

The cats trilled from the corner of the kitchen where they sat with Violet listening to the conversation.

Ellie nodded. "I love running the B and B and I'd love representing the area. Maybe I need to split into two so I can do both."

"That would be way too much work." Courtney shook her head.

Josh came in carrying Gigi and the little girl smiled and reached out her arms when she saw her mother. Angie hugged her and kissed the top of her head.

"Ellie has good news," Angie told Josh after they shared a kiss.

"Are you engaged?" Josh looked excited and everyone chuckled.

"No, I'm not," Ellie told him.

"Oh, too bad. I was looking forward to a wedding."

148

"It's professional news." Ellie explained about the opportunity.

"Congratulations. What a wonderful compliment." Josh smiled at his sister-in-law. "You'd do a terrific job."

Angie rocked her daughter in her arms. "I think it's time to put someone to bed."

Ellie said, "That sounds good to me. I'm going up to my room, clear my head, and read for a while. I'll think everything over tomorrow."

"Good night, all." Josh, Angie, and Gigi headed upstairs to their suite of rooms for the night.

The next afternoon, Chief Martin called Angie to see if she would accompany him to Boston to speak with someone who had worked at the architectural firm with Rachel. No one else in the family could go, so the chief picked her up and they went to the city themselves.

Twenty-nine years old, Kim Michaels was tall with long black hair. She was an architect and a friend of Rachel. The chief had interviewed the owners of the firm along with some of Rachel's colleagues, but no one had pointed him to Kim until the administrative assistant emailed him with the suggestion he speak with her.

Meeting in a coffee shop in downtown Boston, Angie and the chief spotted the woman immediately and went to sit with her.

"It was more than a shock to hear what happened to Rachel. First, she was missing and I had so much hope she'd be found safe. Then, I found out she was dead. An icy chill goes through me whenever I think of her."

A waitress came over and took their orders.

"You met Rachel at work?" Angie asked.

"Yeah. She was great, so helpful to me when I first started. I'd been working at a small firm and I felt overwhelmed at the large company. Rachel showed me the ropes and answered my questions. I think I would have left if not for her."

"You became friends," Angie said.

"We were friends, yes, but we didn't do a lot together outside of work. I live in the city and Rachel lived up the coast in Sweet Cove. She didn't usually want to linger after work. Partly because we worked long hours and she just wanted to go home when we were done. She liked living outside the city. She liked the peace and quiet and being by the shore. Rachel started working more from home, three or four days a week." Kim's face changed to an expression of dismay. "If she didn't live in a such an isolated house, maybe she'd still be alive."

Chief Martin asked, "Did you see her less after she started working from home more often?"

"No, that's when we started doing things together after work. On the days she came into the firm, we'd go to dinner afterward or we'd take a long walk around the neighborhoods. A couple of times we went to a baseball game. I missed seeing her when she decided to do more work from home. She said she missed me, too, so we made sure to connect whenever we could."

"When was the last time you saw her?" the chief questioned.

"Oh, it was about three weeks before she went missing. She was supposed to come in to work a couple of days before she disappeared, but she changed her mind about it. Then I heard what happened, and honestly, I almost passed out."

"Did Rachel confide anything to you about someone she might be having trouble with? A disagreement, a complaining client, someone who was bothering her?"

Kim looked down at the table and didn't say

anything for a minute, and then the waitress brought the beverages over and set them down.

The chief leaned slightly forward. "Do you know of someone Rachel was having issues with?"

After taking a deep breath, Kim lifted her mug and took a long drink. "Sometimes Rachel complained about that guy she was seeing. He was always busy. She would have liked to see him more. She also complained about her sister, Rebecca. Rebecca was always crying poverty to Rachel. Rebecca never seemed like she was all that nice to Rachel. Rachel often gave her money to help out with whatever bills her sister was nagging her about. I didn't think it was fair. Rebecca would blow her money on stuff and then wanted Rachel to bail her out. Rebecca got angry with Rachel for some reason and the two hadn't been talking."

"So Rachel didn't feel close to her sister?"

"I wouldn't say so, but Rachel was always kind and giving. She told me Rebecca was a pain, but she didn't want to hurt her feelings."

The chief was about to ask another question, when Kim cleared her throat. "Rachel told me something that she made me swear I'd never tell anyone about."

The little hairs on Angie's arms stood up.

"Now that she's gone, I suppose my promise doesn't matter anymore." Kim looked to Angie and the chief. "Does it?"

Angie said, "If you think it would be helpful to the investigation, then I think it's okay to tell what you know."

Kim clutched her hands together. "Right before she died, Rachel received death threats."

16

Angie's eyes bugged at Kim's statement.

The chief straightened. "How did she receive the threats? What did they say?"

"She found them in her mailbox. The messages were scrawled in crayon on a piece of paper. One said, *Keep out of my life. Don't go to the police or you'll end up six feet under*. The other said, *Enjoy the next few days. They'll be your last*."

"When did she get the messages?"

"A few days before she disappeared." Kim's eyes watered.

"Did you see the notes?"

"No, she described them to me. Rachel was supposed to come to work for a few days that week, but she decided to stay home. She told me where she found the notes, what they looked like, and what they said. I told her to go to the police with it."

"She didn't?"

"She told me she'd burned them," Kim said. "She was so angry over it. She felt violated so she destroyed them. She wanted them gone. I was disappointed that she did that. It was evidence, but I understand why she got rid of them."

"Did she have any idea who might have sent them?" Worry was etched on Angie's face.

"She didn't. She couldn't think of anyone who had reason to threaten her. And the note said not to go to the police. Rachel was afraid someone was watching her. She was afraid to alert the police about the threat."

"Were those the only threats she received? No phone calls? No more notes?" the chief asked.

"Nothing else that I know of." Kim wiped at her eyes. "I should have insisted she go to the police. Or I should have called and reported it myself."

"Rachel wouldn't have wanted you to do that," Angie said. "It would be easy to consider the threats were a prank. No one could have predicted what happened."

"Did Rachel tell anyone else that she'd received the notes?"

Kim shook her head. "I don't think she did. She wanted to forget about it."

"I've requested the firm provide a list of clients Rachel was working with before her death. I'll go through them again in case one of them is responsible for the threats," Chief Martin said. "Did Rachel ever mention feeling afraid of anyone?"

"She didn't, no." Kim sighed. "I wish her dog was still alive. Maybe Violet could have warned her when someone showed up at the house. Maybe she would have barked. Maybe she would have attacked the person. Rachel loved that dog. She was heartbroken when Violet died. Heartbroken isn't a strong enough description of how she felt. She was devastated. If Violet had been alive, she might have been able to help save Rachel."

"How did Violet die?" Angie asked.

"Violet was diabetic, and the insulin wasn't helping anymore. She'd started having seizures. She had a seizure one day and died in Rachel's arms."

Angie's heart tightened with sadness. "That's terrible. The poor dog. Poor Rachel."

The next morning Angie was back in the bake shop working the counter while her employees made drinks, plated desserts and baked goods, served the customers, and kept the cases and cooler full. The shop was busy all day and many of the locals were discussing the murders of the two women who had been friends for decades.

Angie overheard theories that the women were involved in a drug ring, were smuggling stolen goods, had been secret agents, or had been sheltering international fugitives. All of the suggestions were wrong, but Angie appreciated the creativity of the ideas and looked forward to sharing them with her family later in the day.

When she was wiping down the tables and preparing to close, one of her regular customers came into the bakery. Tori Brothers looked tired and just plain worn out. Angie hadn't seen her for over a week and had wondered if she'd been ill.

"Tori. Hi," Angie greeted the woman warmly. "I don't usually see you in the afternoon. How are things?"

"Hi, Angie. I've been busy with a bunch of stuff. I've taken on new clients so I'm busier than usual. And money's tight. I can't justify splurging on a coffee shop drink every day."

"I'm glad to see you. What can I get for you?"

"The usual. A protein smoothie. I could use a pick me up. I still have four more clients before the end of the day." Tori took a seat at the counter and watched Angie prepare her drink with fresh berries, milk, cocoa powder, and vanilla. "That sure looks good."

While Angie made the smoothie, she kept her attention and focus on the intentions she was putting into the drink … stamina, hope, positive energy, and resilience.

"Here you go." The smoothie had sliced strawberries and a sprinkle of ground chocolate on top. "Would you like a cover on it?"

"Yes, please. I wanted to come by to tell you we're moving."

Angie's face showed surprise at the news.

"I can't keep up with the mortgage payments and the property taxes. Dan borrowed heavily against the house so I don't have much equity. I have to sell it. I don't want to, but I have no choice. Everything in Sweet Cove is too expensive for me to buy and the rents are high, too. I hoped to be able to keep the kids in the same school, but it just isn't possible. We're going to live with my sister for a while. Thank heavens my sister and I get along and the kids love her. It will help me save money so I can get back on my feet. Dan didn't have any life insurance and I don't have much in the way of savings. My sister lives two towns over. I'll be able to keep all my clients, but my route to their houses will be different coming from my sister's place and I won't be passing your shop anymore. And anyway, I can't spend money on little luxuries like smoothies."

"I'm sorry to see you go," Angie told her. "Come by once in a while if you can."

Tori nodded. "If only Sweet Cove had some small affordable houses. I love this town. My kids do, too. It just isn't possible for us to stay under the circumstances."

When she began rustling through her bag for her wallet, Angie waved her off.

"It's on the house."

"You can't do that. You did the same thing the last time I was here."

"It's okay. It's a thank you from me to you. You've been a good customer. I'll miss you."

Tori blinked a few times. "I appreciate it. I'll come back some day and let you know how things are going for us."

"I'd love to hear about it. Take care, Tori."

With a heavy heart, Angie watched the woman leave the bake shop.

When everyone was in bed and the house was quiet, Angie, in her pajamas, and Violet came downstairs to sit in the sunroom for a while. They'd been doing this each night for several days. It gave Angie a chance to think over the facts and details of the crimes without being disturbed, and she enjoyed the time sitting with Violet. She had no idea how the spirit world worked, but she knew Violet was with them and she didn't need to know anything more.

Violet cuddled close and Angie ran her hand over the ghost dog. She still couldn't feel the dog except for some occasional tingling in her fingers, but Violet loved the petting.

"The cases are proving difficult. There isn't a whole lot to go on, but we're not giving up. Things are just going at a snail's pace." She told the dog about the death threat notes and talked about who might have left them. "Really, this is all speculation. We don't know who might have put those awful notes in Rachel's mailbox."

Angie looked out the big windows at the dark night and sighed.

"Rachel's work friend told me how you died. I'm sorry you didn't have more time on earth. I saw that Rachel kept your picture and your collar on her mantle. The friend said that Rachel loved you very much."

The dog leaned her head against Angie's leg.

"You both left the earth too soon."

Closing her eyes for a few minutes, Angie let her mind wander over the aspects of the murders. Occasionally, something would float by that seemed important, but then it would fade and disappear. It was like trying to catch and hold some mist that was moving in the air. Although both Angie's and Jenna's paranormal skills had strengthened after the birth of their daughters, in this case, their abilities didn't seem as sharp for some reason. Angie thought about talking to Orla about it, or maybe she could speak to a friend with strong skills they'd met last summer who lived close by in the town of Hamlet.

Angie also wanted to inspect Mr. Finch's painting for any hidden clues it might hold. She'd remember to do that in the morning. She held suspicions about Rachel's sister, Rebecca, and the boyfriend, Jason, the park ranger and photographer. Something about them seemed off, but it might only be that their relationships with Rachel weren't strong.

Angie would be returning to New Hampshire soon to talk to Jessica's friend, Amy Windfall. They'd been friends since high school and Angie hoped the woman would have some insight on Jessica's murder and the crime connection between Jessica and Rachel.

Angie said to the dog, "Someone, somewhere, knows a little thing that will break this double-murder case wide open. I just have to find that link and it will lead us to the answers."

Pushing herself up from the sofa, Angie stretched and yawned. "Come on, sweet Violet. It's time for bed."

17

The kitchen buzzed with activity as everyone helped prepare dinner. Chicken pot pies and vegetable pot pies were baking in the oven while the sisters were busy making the side dishes and desserts. Courtney and Mr. Finch chopped broccoli, cabbage, red onion, pecans, and raisins for the broccoli slaw. Ellie made a fruit salad and a green salad, Jenna mixed ingredients for the cornbread, and Angie frosted an apple spice cake with maple buttercream frosting while a dark chocolate pear cake cooled on a wire rack.

"I think we have too much food." Ellie looked around at all the work being done.

"There can never be too much food." Mr. Finch grinned. "This way we can have leftovers."

"For days," Courtney smiled and reached for another onion.

Occasionally lifting their noses in the air to inhale the scents, the cats and Violet rested together on a big comfy cat bed in the corner of the room. Gigi and Libby played on a blanket on the floor next to the cats.

The four men came into the kitchen within minutes of each other. Rufus brought a bouquet of flowers for the table, Josh had picked up beer and wine, Tom made a cranberry sauce, and Jack brought a tray of corn on the cob with Cotija cheese.

When the food was ready, it was carried to the dining room table and everyone took their seats. Josh and Tom put their daughters in highchairs next to them.

"What a great idea. This is going to be a fun night," Rufus wore a big smile.

"Where's Betty?" Tom asked Finch.

"Miss Betty had to work this evening. She might join us later."

"And what about Chief Martin and Lucille?" Josh asked.

"They wanted a quiet evening at home together," Angie explained.

"That's understandable," Finch nodded. "Phillip

has been straight out on the double murder case. It's good for him to relax at home."

The group discussed their days. Tom, who owned a construction and renovation business, told them about a new antique Colonial home his company had recently signed to renovate. The place dated back to the late 1700s and he was eager to get to work on it. Rufus and Jack talked about a free seminar on estate planning they were preparing to offer the public. They'd be giving the talk at senior centers on the North Shore to help people prepare their long-term health planning, wealth preservation, and transfer of assets.

"You don't have to be wealthy to come to the seminar," Rufus said. "It's designed to help everyone with estate planning."

"That sounds very interesting," Finch said.

Josh told the group about a new wing being built at the resort and about all the weddings, conferences, and special events being booked through June of next year. "We've never had so many events booked so far in advance. I might need to hire another event planner to help out with all the business."

Finch and Courtney reported that the candy

shop was busier than any September so far and described some new candy ideas they had.

"We'll bring some samples home to get your opinions on them," Courtney told them.

"It's a heavy burden to have to try new candies," Tom kidded, "but someone has to do it."

Jenna told them about the new jewelry line she was designing for the winter collection and that she'd already received a huge order from a Boston department store.

Angie said, "The bake shop was really busy today. It seems like more and more people are extending their vacations late into September. The town is mobbed and people are even going in the water." She went on to tell them about Tori Brothers who would be selling her house due to problems with her finances.

"She's the one whose husband passed away unexpectedly?" Courtney asked.

"That's her. There was no life insurance and she's having trouble paying the mortgage and taxes on her one salary," Angie explained. "She's moving in with her sister for a while. She'd love to stay in town, but there's nothing affordable here."

Ellie and Jack exchanged glances with one another.

"That's really too bad," Jenna said. "There should be more housing options in town. I'm sure there are a lot of older people who'd like to downsize and stay in Sweet Cove, but there aren't enough smaller houses or townhouses for them."

After dessert was served and enjoyed, the group cleaned up and then went outside to the backyard. Josh got the fire pit going while Tom pushed the wheelbarrow full of pumpkins to the patio table under the pergola. The lattice work and the beams and poles of the pergola were wrapped with tiny orange lights. Rufus and Jack lit the tiki torches and soon the yard was full of light.

Pumpkin carving kits were scattered over the tabletop along with pipe cleaners, feathers, buttons, and ribbons and everyone went to the wheelbarrow to choose a pumpkin to carve.

Gigi and Libby sat on a blanket with their toys, and the cats and Violet sat next to them watching.

Ellie came out of the house with a tray of hot chocolates and hot toddies. Courtney brought out bowls of popcorn and pretzels.

Then they all set to carving their pumpkins. Some were scary, some funny, and some were pretty. Angie made a face like a woman on hers and used multi-colored pipe cleaners stuck all over the top and back for her hair. Tom carved a tiger, Josh created a bird, and Mr. Finch carved a silhouette of a witch into his and when he put the candle inside it backlit the design beautifully.

Courtney carved holes all around her pumpkin so the candlelight would shine through, then she painted it white. Rufus cut a haunted house into his, and Jack made a face on his pumpkin and carved out a bow tie on it, too. Jenna made a woman's face on hers and carved a pearl necklace around the neck. Ellie cut out lines like flames from the bottom of her pumpkin to the top and when the candle went inside, it looked like the pumpkin was on fire.

They set all of them along the top of the stonewall and stood behind them for a photo, then they gathered around the fire pit to sip drinks, roast marshmallows, and nibble on popcorn.

Tom rubbed his stomach. "I'm about to explode. I should slow down, but everything tastes so good."

Jenna looked over at Ellie. "You haven't told us what you've been thinking about running for state representative. Have you made any decisions yet?"

Ellie and Jack shared a glance.

"I think I've made my decision."

All eyes were glued to Ellie.

"I'm going to decline the offer of support to run."

"Oh man," Courtney sounded disappointed. "Why did you decide not to run?"

"I love running the bed and breakfast and I didn't want to be away from home so much. If I won the seat, I'd have to be in Boston a lot and I'd be out most evenings at meetings. I don't want to do that right now. I want to be with my family."

"Good for you, Ellie," Angie said.

"But I do want to be of service to others," Ellie added.

"So we put our heads together," Jack told them, "and we came up with a project proposal that we think would enhance life in Sweet Cove for a lot of people."

"What's this about?" Josh questioned, eager to hear.

"There's a large piece of land for sale near the state park," Ellie said. "It's about fifteen acres in size. Jack and I want to buy it and plan a neighborhood of smaller homes like Capes and ranches, along with some townhouses. Some of the land will be kept as a park with walking and biking trails winding through the space. The homes will be affordable and manageable in size for a single person, a couple, or a small family."

Jack said, "As Angie pointed out when she told us

about her customer who lost her husband and couldn't make ends meet, there are a lot of people who either grew up in Sweet Cove and want to move back, couples looking to downsize, single people who want a small house, or someone who has had a financial setback, but wants to stay in town."

"The project would be helpful to the community. I want to do things that benefit the town and the people." Ellie looked around the small group. "We aren't out to make a bundle of money. We'd only make a very small profit to cover our time. We'd like to work with a bank in town that would offer low-interest loans so the houses will be affordable."

"I think it's a wonderful idea, Miss Ellie," Finch smiled. "You could buy that land and build huge houses on it and probably make a million dollars or more of profit. I'm impressed with your concern for others."

"We're going to have to beat out some developers who want to do just that," Jack said. "We're taking our plans to the bank in a few days to see if we can get backing."

"I really hope it works out," Ellie said.

"I like the idea so much," Finch said, "that I would like to invest in the project."

"Really?" Ellie's eyes went wide.

"We can talk about the particulars tomorrow if you like," Finch said.

"I'd like to be part of that meeting as well," Josh said. "As long as Angie is onboard, I think we'd like to invest in it, too." He looked to his wife.

"I think it's a great idea," Angie told them.

"And not to be left out," Tom said, "I'd be happy to volunteer as a contract consultant helping with the design and overlooking the work being done. For free."

"Wow," Ellie looked like she was going to cry. "I never expected this."

"You know what?" Courtney asked. "I think this idea is a whole lot better than being a state representative."

Ellie laughed.

"And you know we'll all help out in any way we can," Courtney added. "I'm proud of you ... both of you." She looked from her sister to Jack.

Euclid trilled from his position on a lounge chair near the fire pit.

"What's the neighborhood going to be called?" Josh asked.

Ellie smiled again. "Roseland."

18

It was late afternoon when Angie stood behind the counter with Louisa, the woman who had worked with her for a couple of years and who now managed the museum bake shop Angie owned. They were discussing new additions to the menu for the fall and winter seasons. Soup and chili were at the top of the list for lunchtime selections and different pie flavors were being considered.

"Something more substantial and hearty would be good," Louisa suggested. Her long black hair with blue tinted ends had been swept up into a bun. "What about apple-spice Bundt cake? Or the autumn fruit pie?"

"Those sound good," Angie agreed. "I'll bake

them tonight and ask the family to taste test. I was thinking about a Nutella-s'mores pie."

"Ooh, that sounds yummy."

"I'll try to make that one tonight, too. I'll bring them down to the museum bake shop so you can try them," Angie said.

The door opened and Chief Martin walked over to the counter. "Afternoon."

The women greeted him and Angie brought over a black coffee and a slice of warm apple pie with caramel sauce.

The three of them chatted for a while until Louisa had to leave to return to the museum. "See you tomorrow," she told Angie.

Leaning forward and keeping her voice down, Angie asked the chief, "Is there some news?"

"Some. Not much. I spoke with Rachel's sister, Rebecca. She doesn't have an alibi for the time Rachel was attacked."

A frown pulled at the corners of Angie's mouth. "Where does she say she was?"

"At home. The high school where she teaches gets out at 2:15pm. She could have easily driven here in time to commit the attack on Rachel. It would fit the timeline we got from the coroner."

"Rebecca told us she and Rachel hadn't talked for about six months. I wonder if she went to talk to her sister, maybe she wanted to make amends, but things didn't go well and they got into an argument, and then Rebecca attacked her." Angie thought of something. "What about her phone records? They'd show if Rebecca was in the Sweet Cove area at the time of the crime."

"Her phone was off during the afternoon." The chief's face was expressionless. "She claims to turn it off when she's at school, and she forgot to turn it back on when she got home."

"That's convenient."

"Isn't it?"

"It could be the truth," Angie said.

"And it might not be." Chief Martin ate some of the pie. "This is really good."

"What will you do now?"

"We can try to get highway toll information to see if Rebecca's car was on the highway that afternoon."

"She could have taken back roads," Angie surmised.

"Yeah, that would have lengthened the trip here though. If she drove the back way, it would have taken a little over an hour to get here. It's still within the window of possibility."

"Although, I don't see why she wouldn't take the highway if she was simply going to see Rachel to try and make amends," Angie noted. "She had nothing to hide. She was going to visit her sister. The crime didn't seem premeditated. The attack might have been the result of an escalation in anger. Rebecca could have argued with Rachel, lost it, and grabbed the knife. It's easy to make a case for it happening that way."

"Right. But what about Jessica's murder?" the chief asked. "We think the crimes are linked. What would have been Rebecca's motivation to kill Jessica?"

"Maybe Rebecca thought Rachel told Jessica something damning about her. She might have been afraid she'd lose her job if the information came out."

"I can see the attack on Rachel happening due to sudden rage," the chief said. "But I'm having trouble tying Rebecca to a planned homicide. It would have to be something pretty big for her to kill two people over it."

"Time will tell," Angie nodded. "If she did it, you'll find the evidence."

"Eventually." The chief shook his head. "I may be well into my nineties before that happens."

Angie chuckled. "You'd better hurry up and figure it out then. Time flies. You'll be in your nineties before you know it," she kidded.

The chief just scowled.

"What about the boyfriend, Jason Field? Is there anything new on him? Was he in the state park at the time of the attack?"

"People saw him in the park, but no one saw him there around the time of the crime."

"So another person who doesn't have an alibi?"

"That's right."

"What would have been his motive?" Angie asked.

"Unknown." The chief finished his last bite of the pie. "Don't tell Lucille I ate that. She'll skin me. I'm supposed to be improving my health habits."

Angie leveled her eyes at the chief. "You should have told me that before I brought you a slice."

"It slipped my mind," the chief grinned.

When the chief left, Angie told her employees they could leave early. She felt like having some time to herself and didn't mind cleaning up and preparing for the next day's business on her own so she locked the door and started in on the tasks, all the while thinking about the murders.

Angie wanted to inspect Mr. Finch's farmhouse painting, but the man asked her to wait until his revisions were complete. He felt a finished work would provide more clues than something partially done. She didn't want to wait, but knew Finch was probably right.

If Rebecca's phone had been off unintentionally, it would be an unfortunate coincidence since it cast suspicion on the woman. And there was something about the boyfriend that Angie didn't like. Something seemed missing in his responses to her questions, but it may only have been because the young man wasn't invested in his relationship with Rachel.

She finished cleaning and checking that everything was ready for the morning rush, and then she went to the cooler and took out the boxes of pastries and desserts ordered by the Pirate's Den Restaurant in the middle of town. Angie had been supplying the popular restaurant with baked goods for two years and the owners had become good friends.

She checked the invoice against the boxes, and satisfied the order was complete, she started carrying the goods out to Ellie's van for transport to the restaurant. Angie often borrowed her sister's van to make deliveries around town and she was sure to fill it with gas when she was done.

In less than ten minutes, Angie pulled the van to the curb right in front of the restaurant. She loaded up the boxes and headed for the entrance.

"I saw you coming." Bessie Lindquist held the door open for the young woman, and took a few boxes from the top of the stack. "Did we order all of this?" she laughed. Bessie and her husband had owned the restaurant for over twenty years. The woman had silver-blond hair cut short in layers around her friendly face. She always was upbeat and positive and she loved running the place.

"The customers love your pies and cakes and everything else. We could never replace you. You're the best baker we've ever contracted with."

Some of the waitstaff came over to get the boxes and they carried them into the kitchen as Angie placed the invoice on the counter.

"Want a cup of coffee?"

"Sure. A quick one. I need to get home to see my little one."

"How's she doing? Must be getting big." Bessie

carried a mug of coffee over along with a pot of cream.

Angie smiled. "She sure is. She's saying words and crawling. She stands up and holds on to the coffee table and looks like she's going to walk across the room. She hasn't done it yet, but she's on her way. Libby is doing all the same things. I think they urge each other on. When one does something, the other starts doing it, too."

"My twins were like that when they were growing up. In some ways it seems like yesterday, and in other ways, it feels like a hundred years ago." Bessie leaned against the counter with a faraway look in her eyes.

"The past months have flown by. If that's any indication, I know the years will fly by, too. I need to hang on to my little girl. I don't want her to grow up so fast." Angie sipped her coffee while Bessie signed the invoice.

"Isn't it so awful about Rachel Princeton?" Bessie asked. "I knew her a little. She used to come in for dinner at least once a week. I enjoyed talking with her. She was quite the well-known architect."

"I just learned that about her. Who did she come in with?"

"Rachel came by herself a lot. She told me she

didn't mind eating alone. It gave her mind a chance to relax. Sometimes, she came in with her boyfriend, Jason. Once in a while, with a friend. A few times with her sister. I don't remember her name."

"Rebecca," Angie told her.

"That's right. They hadn't been in together for months, and then I saw the sister just the other day. She came in to grab a bite."

"Rebecca was staying at the B and B for two nights right after Rachel went missing," Angie explained.

"It wasn't *after* Rachel disappeared when Rebecca was in here," Bessie said. "Rebecca was here on the day Rachel was attacked."

Angie's heart rate sped up. "She was? What time was that? Do you remember?"

"It was around 2:30pm. It's always slow around that time. It's after the lunch crowd and too early for the dinner business. She told me she left school early because she had the last block of the day free. She was going to visit Rachel after she had something to eat."

"How long did she stay?"

"Not long. She didn't have a meal, only a slice of pie and a cup of coffee. She told me she hadn't seen her sister for quite a while. She was looking forward to catching up."

Rebecca was on her way to see Rachel? That was right around the time Rachel was attacked.

Angie's head was spinning.

"I *was* in Sweet Cove that afternoon," Rebecca Princeton Wallace told Angie and Chief Martin. "I wanted to talk to Rachel. I thought it would be better to speak face to face. I told you I was at home because I was afraid you'd try to tie me to the murder."

It was late afternoon and Angie, Chief Martin, and Violet sat in Rebecca's dining room in Hollis, New Hampshire. The chief would be asking most of the questions while Angie watched and listened ... and sensed whatever she could. Rebecca couldn't see the ghost dog and had no idea she was there.

"Don't you teach at the high school until 2:30pm?" the chief questioned the woman.

"I had a preparation block during the last period

of the school day," Rebecca explained. "We're allowed to leave the school campus during our preparation time."

"You don't have to handle the homeroom right before the close of school?"

"The students leave for the buses from their last block class." Rebecca's face looked tense and anxious. "So I took the opportunity to leave early."

What route did you take to Sweet Cove?" Chief Martin wanted to know.

"I took the route that runs along the coast. I didn't feel like taking the highway. I wasn't in a hurry. In fact, I was dreading the visit. The longer drive gave me time to think about what I was going to say to my sister."

"Did Rachel know you were coming?"

Rebecca shook her head. "No, I thought she'd refuse to see me. I thought if I showed up on her doorstep then maybe she'd talk to me."

"What if she wasn't at home?" the chief asked.

"Rachel always worked until at least 6pm. I was pretty sure she'd be at home. There was the chance she went into the city to work at the office, but at the end of the week, she usually stayed in Sweet Cove and didn't make the trip into Boston."

"What did you want to talk to her about?"

Violet pinned her gaze on the woman.

Rebecca looked down at the tabletop. "I wanted us to make up. I didn't want to be estranged from her anymore. Look, I've been jealous of Rachel since she was born. She was the smartest, the prettiest, the hardest worker. My parents preferred Rachel to me. It made me resentful. I was average, Rachel was a superstar. I've been thinking about it all for a few months. I shouldn't have taken my resentment out on my sister. Rachel was always good to me."

"When you got to Sweet Cove, what did you do?" the chief asked.

"I drove around for a while. I was nervous about seeing Rachel." Rebecca let out a long breath. "I decided to go to the restaurant not far from Rachel's house. It's called the Pirate's Den. Rachel and I went there a few times. I got coffee and some dessert and I just sat there for a while thinking about my sister. What would I do if she didn't want to see me? How would I feel? Would the hurt of rejection send me into a downward spiral? When it came to Rachel, my self-esteem always took a nosedive. Her accomplishments made me feel like I was a loser."

"So what did you decide to do?" Angie asked while watching the woman's expression and body language.

"I decided to come home to Hollis. I couldn't face it." Rebecca's eyes filled up. "I needed more time to think about trying to rekindle a relationship. But we know how that worked out. Rachel's gone. She didn't know I wanted to make amends. She'll never know that I cared about her and that I wanted to put the past in the past and start over."

"Did you drive by your sister's house?" Angie spoke kindly.

"I didn't." Rebecca swallowed hard. "I should have. If I was there, the attacker might have gone away. Rachel might still be alive. But I didn't go to see her. I'm a coward."

Angie leaned forward. "You can't blame yourself. If you were there and scared off the killer, he would have returned another time."

Violet turned to Angie, and then back to Rebecca.

"Maybe." Rebecca passed her hand over her eyes. "I don't know."

"If we access your phone records, will they tell us that you took the slower route to Sweet Cove?" the chief asked. "Will the records show you didn't ride by Rachel's house?" The chief had already pulled the phone records and discovered that the phone was off during the afternoon. He wanted to see what Rebecca would say under duress.

"I told you before." Rebecca stiffened. "I always turn my phone off while I'm teaching and sometimes I forget to turn it back on. That's why my phone was off that day. I didn't remember to turn it on. I wasn't trying to hide my whereabouts."

Chief Martin nodded. "I need to ask the next question ... are you having financial difficulties?"

Rebecca's eyes widened and her mouth opened as if she was about to say something, but then she shut it and stared at the chief. "Why are you asking me that?"

"Because it's possible that you were going to see Rachel about a loan."

Angie looked at Rebecca and then turned to the chief.

"I ... I wanted to repair our relationship," Rebecca stammered.

"In addition to needing money." The chief made it a statement, not a question.

The woman began to get huffy. "My sister was important to me."

"Are you having a problem with gambling?"

One of Angie's eyebrows raised.

"What? What kind of a question is that?" Rebecca blinked fast and looked across the room.

"I believe you are heavily in debt due to gambling. For many, many thousands." The chief let the comment sink in.

"That's not why I went to see Rachel." Rebecca folded her arms over her chest.

The chief shot off questions in quick succession. "After you left the Pirate's Den, did you go to your sister's house? Did Rachel refuse to give you a loan? Did you become enraged? Did you grab a weapon from the kitchen counter?"

"No, no. I did not." Rebecca was practically screeching. "That's not what happened. I didn't see Rachel that day. I swear it."

"Were you going to ask her for money?"

"Yes." Rebecca's shoulders trembled. "I admit it. But I didn't go to her house."

"Why not?"

"Because I chickened out."

Outside standing by the cars, Angie and the chief discussed the interview.

"I don't know if I believe her," the chief admitted.

"I don't know either. There's something simmering under the surface," Angie said. "It's most likely a deep resentment toward her sister. That flows off Rebecca in waves. But did her resentment lead to murder? I'm not sure."

Violet rubbed her head against Angie's leg.

"It's possible. I don't know if I buy her forgetting to turn on her phone when she left school." Chief Martin took a quick glance to Rebecca's house. "She stays on the suspect list, for now anyway."

"I agree."

"Are you still going to see Jessica's friend?"

"I thought I may as well since I'm in New Hampshire already," Angie said. "I want to talk to her."

"Well, good luck with it. She wasn't that forthcoming with me when I met with her."

"I'll see what I can weasel out of her." Angie smiled.

"Hopefully, more than I could. I'll see you back in Sweet Cove." The chief went to his car to head back home for a meeting.

Angie and Violet drove to Amy Windfall's house which turned out to be only two blocks away from her deceased friend's home.

Inside the house, Angie sat with the young

woman at the kitchen table while Violet sat in a corner of the room.

Amy was thirty years old, petite and slim with white blond hair cut in a boyish bob. She was an assistant manager of one of the banks in Hollis and had known Jessica Hanson for years.

"It almost knocked me to the ground when Jessica's sister called me to tell me what happened. For a few seconds, I couldn't even breathe." Amy lifted her eyes to Angie. "I loved Jess. She was so inspiring. She had so much drive and ambition. She always gave me good advice when I asked her questions about business and management."

"Did you know Rachel Princeton?" Angie asked.

"Sure, I'd known her since high school. I liked her. We didn't take many of the same classes so I wasn't as close to her as I was to Jess. Rachel was super smart. I always knew she'd make something of herself." Amy shifted around uncomfortably. "Why would someone kill both of them? It freaks me out."

"Did Jessica say anything to you about being worried about someone?"

Violet watched the woman's face.

"No, she didn't. She didn't tell me about anything unusual."

"Is there anyone you feel suspicious about?"

Amy brushed a strand of hair back from her face. "Nobody will know what I say to you, right? You're not recording this?"

"I have to write a report for Chief Martin summarizing what we talked about. He's the investigator on the case. I can't keep things from him," Angie explained.

"I don't mean him. I mean regular people. Citizens of the town won't see your report, will they?"

"Definitely not. Is there someone in particular you're worried about?" A flutter of unease ran down Angie's arms.

"Well, I don't like Jess's old boyfriend. His name is Andrew Nystrom. He's bossy and never treated Jess very well. He thinks he's great. He thinks everyone should fall in love with him. I can't stand him," Amy said.

"Do you think he had something to do with Jessica's death?"

"I don't know. They hadn't been getting along. He accused Jess of cheating on him. She didn't. Jess would never do that. He went on and on about it and Jess got sick of his distrust so she ended the relationship. He didn't like that."

"Did he threaten her?"

"Not in so many words. He called her one night

when he was drunk. He said a lot of terrible things to her." Amy shook her head. "I told her to report him to the police, but she wouldn't do it."

"When did she break up with him?"

"The week before Rachel came to visit."

"Do you know what kind of a car he drives?"

"Yeah. One of those trucks everyone drives. An F-150."

Violet gave Angie a look of concern.

20

Angie continued the interview with Amy Windfall. "I'll have Chief Martin look into it. When the chief spoke with you, did you tell him about Jessica's boyfriend and their breakup?"

"I didn't tell him. I didn't think it was relevant to Jessica's murder. I thought the killer had to be someone who had a connection to both Jessica and Rachel."

"I understand. I'll let the chief know. If he decides it could be important, then he'll look into it. Do you know what Rachel and Jessica did during the weekend Rachel came up?"

"I know they rode bikes on the rail trail," Amy recalled. "Went out for dinner, took a hike. I met them in a pub one night. We had a fun time."

"Did they meet up with other friends?" Angie questioned.

"I'm not sure. There were a few of us at the pub together. I don't know if they met up with other people while Rachel was here." Amy's face looked worried. "Do you think the killer is choosing his victims from the people who went to school here in town? Rachel and Jess were in the same class. Do you think the rest of us are in danger?"

Angie hadn't considered the idea. "I'm not sure if Chief Martin is looking into that, but I haven't heard the suggestion floating around. I think that's a long shot."

"Okay." Amy appeared relieved to hear law enforcement wasn't actively considering that members of a certain high school class were being targeted. "Oh, I remember Jess and Rachel took a drive to the state line one evening. Rachel had a client there and the person wanted her to come that weekend to talk to her about a renovation. Rachel was annoyed about it, but they went anyway."

"Do you know what town they went to?"

"I think it was Eastford," Amy said.

"Did you see the women after you went to the pub together?"

"I didn't." Amy sighed. "That was the last time I ever saw them."

Angie and Violet got into the car, but before they left, Angie texted the chief to ask if he knew of any clients Rachel had near the Massachusetts or New Hampshire line, possibly in Eastford. After pulling onto the highway to head home, Angie asked Violet what she thought of the interviews with Rachel's sister and the friend, Amy.

Violet, sitting in the front passenger seat ... which Angie okayed because if there was an accident, the ghost dog couldn't sustain any injuries ... looked at the young woman and then faced front to watch out the window.

"That's what I thought, too." Angie moved the vehicle into the right lane. "Not much to go on. Rebecca told us a plausible story, but did she make the whole thing up? She left school early, left her cell phone off, went to Sweet Cove supposedly to convince her sister to salvage their relationship, but really to ask for a loan. But she got cold feet and decided to go home instead. The chief told me Rebecca has a lot of debt from gambling. Did Rachel refuse to talk to her sister or did she refuse to give Rebecca a loan? Did Rebecca become infuriated and kill Rachel?" Angie shook her head. "It's possible Rebecca is the killer, but why would she kill Jessica? I can't come up with motivation for that."

Violet gave Angie an encouraging look.

"And Amy didn't really have anything to tell us except about Jessica's boyfriend being a jerk. He was in a rage over being dumped, but would that make him kill Jessica? And if he did, why would he kill Rachel?"

Angie maneuvered the car off the highway and onto a quiet road.

"Maybe there are really two killers and the women's murders aren't connected at all. It could be a terrible coincidence that they were killed within days of one another."

Getting the urge to drive by Rachel's house, Angie turned onto a smaller road that led into Sweet Cove the back way.

"Let's stop by Rachel's. I'd like to stand in the yard for a few minutes."

When they pulled into Rachel's long driveway and approached the house to park near the garage, Angie's heart dropped. A pickup truck was parked in front of the house and it was the same make and model of the vehicle that had left a tire print near the garage.

Not wanting to get out of the car, Angie clutched the steering wheel. "Maybe we should get out of here," she told Violet.

The dog stared at the house.

A man walked around the side of the house heading for his truck. It was Jason Field, Rachel's sort-of boyfriend. He looked surprised that someone else's car was parked in the driveway.

Angie and Violet got out of the car.

"Hey," Jason said when he recognized her.

Angie nodded. "I wasn't expecting to see you here."

"Yeah, well, I let Rachel borrow a lawn seed spreader a while back. I came by to see if it was in the shed."

"It isn't?"

Jason shook his head. "Maybe it's in the basement."

"You can call Chief Martin. He'll probably let you in."

"Maybe I will."

Angie noticed a *for sale* sign in the window of Jason's truck. Something pricked at her skin. *Why was he selling it? Could there be evidence from Rachel's murder inside?* "You're getting rid of your truck?"

"I want a new one."

"It looks new to me."

"It has some issues. It's off warranty. I want to unload it."

"My husband and I would like to get a truck," she fibbed. She wanted to see what he'd say if she showed interest in the vehicle. "Maybe we can come and look at it someday."

"Nah. You don't want it. I don't want to sell it to someone I know. It might be trouble down the line, and then I'd feel bad about selling it to you."

"Really? We'd have it checked out with a mechanic. We wouldn't blame you if something went wrong. Can I look at it?"

"Another time. I have to get going." Jason sure seemed like he didn't want Angie near the truck.

"Maybe I'll give you a call about it," Angie told him.

"Yeah, okay. Do that." Jason turned and hurried to his truck, got in, and drove away.

"Did that seem a little odd to you?" Angie asked Violet.

The dog wagged her tail.

"Or maybe I'm being too suspicious. Come on, Violet, let's go home."

Back at the house, Angie texted the chief to tell him Jason Field was at Rachel's house and that he was selling his truck. She went to the kitchen to find Mr. Finch, Gigi, Libby, Euclid, and Circe playing with toys on the floor.

"Miss Angie," Finch greeted her warmly. "We are having a wonderful game of roll the ball. The girls roll the ball and one of the cats runs to it and bats it back to us. It is most entertaining."

Angie kissed both little girls and sat with them on the blanket while Violet ran over to join the felines. "What a fun game." She rolled one of the balls and Euclid darted after it, stopped it, and gave it a bop with his paw to send it back to where it came from.

With one hand, Finch held onto a chair and with the other clutching his cane, he pushed himself off the floor. "Not as young as I used to be," he grinned.

"But young in spirit," Angie smiled at him.

"Indeed," the man winked. "And this family keeps me so. How was the trip to New Hampshire?

Angie gave Finch the highlights of the interviews and told him about running into Jason Field at Rachel's house. "I'm suspicious of everyone and everything, but my senses don't point to anyone in particular."

"Maybe that's because you have yet to meet the killer," Finch suggested.

"Then who is it? And what was the motivation?" Angie knew the man couldn't answer her questions, she just had to ask them aloud.

"If you discover the motivation, you will most likely discover the killer." Finch headed for the stove. "Cup of tea?"

"I would love that." Angie handed a ball to each little girl and, giggling, they rolled them for the cats to chase.

"Ball!" they each shouted.

"How are you managing with the kids, Mr. Finch? Is taking care of them too much with your leg?"

"I'm fine, Miss Angie. I pick the girls up one at a time and I put them in the double stroller when we move from room to room. It's good for me to be active. It actually helps my leg to feel more nimble. I'm not often alone. Miss Ellie is usually here all day and Miss Jenna is right down the hall in her workshop if I need her."

"The benefits of a large family." Angie smiled.

"The day I found all of you was the luckiest day of my life." Finch handed the young woman a mug of tea. "I've been working on the painting. Would you like to see it?"

Angie, carrying Gigi, Finch, holding Libby, the cats, and Violet walked into the man's sunroom where he'd been doing his painting. The canvas was perched on the easel.

Finch had added more orange and red foliage to the picture, and there was now a white cat sitting on a stone wall. Angie also noticed that the ell off the main building looked dilapidated and ready to keel over.

Starting at the tips of her toes, a tingling sensation moved through her legs, into her torso, to her neck, and into her head, buzzing as it went.

"This picture ... this farmhouse," Angie said softly. "It's a clue. It will lead us to the killer. I know it."

21

It was a warm sunny afternoon when Angie and Ellie, Euclid, Circe, and Violet walked in the open pasture heading to the tree line. Ellie was showing them the land she and Jack wanted to buy for the new neighborhood they hoped to build.

"Back there is where the road would come in." Ellie pointed. "It will loop around in a figure eight. We want to leave as much of the trees and under-brush as possible. That will give people nice back-yards with nature right behind them. Walking trails will loop around behind the houses and some of them will link into the state park trails."

"It's beautiful," Angie admired the acreage. "It sounds like a wonderful neighborhood."

"I hope we can beat out the other bidders." Ellie

looked worried. "The other two people who are interested want to build huge houses with small lots all crammed in together. They'll cut down all the trees. It will be ugly. Jack and I are looking into setting something up on one of those crowd-sourced fundraising sites to help pay for the land. We're going to the bank tomorrow with our ideas and hope we can at least get a loan to buy the land."

"You're both doing a great job with this."

"Do you think I'm being foolish? Am I biting off more than I can chew? Is it dumb to want to make a nice place for people to live that's affordable? Even if we do it, it will only help a small number of people out of the many who need a hand. Am I being too idealistic?"

Angie smiled. "No, you're not being too idealistic. Are you taking on an enormous project? Yup, but so what? You'll have a team of people behind you. You're a natural organizer. Look how well you handle the B and B, from managing the rooms, to working with the guests, to hiring and supervising the cleaning staff. And it isn't possible to help everyone, but you'll be helping some, and that's what matters."

Ellie hugged Angie. "Thanks. You're the best sister."

"Courtney and Jenna might not like to hear that," Angie kidded.

"They're the best sisters, too." Ellie pointed to the far end of the field. "Want to walk along the trails? There's an overlook that gives a really nice view of the whole property."

"Let's go. I'd love to see that."

Euclid, Circe, and Violet ran ahead of the sisters having fun taking turns chasing each other.

"Do you think Violet will stay with us?" Ellie asked as they started to walk the trails. "She's such a nice dog."

"I don't know. I'd be happy if she stayed. I really love her."

"But does she have to cross over?"

"I have no idea how ghosts and spirits work. I wouldn't even know what to ask anyone who *did* know about them. She came to us because she wants us to help find the person who hurt Rachel. If we find the killer, she'll probably leave."

"Don't say *if*, say *when* we find the killer."

They reached the top of the hill and emerged through some trees to see a grand view stretching out below them of the trees, bushes, and meadows.

Angie looked out at the vista. "It's lovely. It will be a beautiful neighborhood when it's done."

The cats trilled and Violet wagged her tail.

Angie's phone buzzed in her pocket. "It's Chief Martin. He wants to know if we're at home."

"Maybe he has some good news." Ellie's voice was hopeful.

"I texted him and told him we're looking at the land."

A reply text came right away.

"He's nearby. He'll meet us at the car when we're done."

"We're done. That's all I wanted to show you. Want to head back?"

After a fifteen-minute walk back to where they left the car at the side of the road, they saw the chief standing by his vehicle waiting for them. The cats and Violet darted over to greet the man.

"I thought I'd give you an update. I got in touch with Jason Field after you told me he was at Rachel's house yesterday. I told him I'd let him into the basement if he wanted to look for the grass seed spreader. We met there this morning. We found the spreader in the cellar. I talked to him about his truck. He let me see inside."

Angie grunted. "Why did he let you look at it, but not me?"

"I'm a cop," the chief deadpanned. "There's

more. Some of the officers found a couple who were in the state park on the afternoon Rachel went missing. They reported that they spoke with Jason Field about where to find some trails they were looking for. The timing would place him in the park at the time of the disappearance. He wouldn't have had time to get to Rachel's house within the window the crime took place."

"Well then, I guess we can cross him off the list," Angie said. "One less person to think about."

"We're also looking into Jessica's former boyfriend, Andrew Nystrom. He's the one who called Jessica when he was drunk and called her some pretty bad names. We'll be talking to him tomorrow and find out if he threatened her. That's all I've got right now."

"At least you've eliminated someone from the suspect list," Ellie said. "You're narrowing it down."

"It feels like we'll never get to the end of this," the chief said. "Gotta keep digging."

Angie put her hand on the man's arm. "We'll get there. I can feel it."

The chief smiled. "Good to know."

When Ellie and Angie returned to the house and went inside, they spotted Finch, Josh, Tom, Jack, and Rufus sitting in the yard together.

"What's going on?" Angie asked as she gazed out of the kitchen window.

"It's the first training session with Mr. Finch," Ellie chuckled. "He's teaching them to be more open to their paranormal abilities."

Courtney came up behind them. "Ha. This should be good."

"Does everyone really have paranormal abilities?" Angie questioned.

"I doubt it," Courtney said, "but I bet there's a whole bunch of people who could sense things if they got some instruction."

Ellie agreed. "There must be different levels of ability across the population."

"Maybe one of the guys will actually have some skills," Angie said.

Jenna came into the kitchen with Gigi and Libby.

"We just got back." Angie took her daughter in her arms and hugged her causing the little girl to giggle.

"Did you see what's going on in the backyard?" Jenna smiled.

"We saw them through the window," Ellie told her. "If we go outside, will we disturb them?"

"Mr. Finch asked me to come out there in twenty minutes. That was twenty minutes ago," Courtney said. "I'll head out. Why don't you come? If they don't want us watching, they'll let us know."

When the women, the girls, the cats, and Violet went into the garden, Courtney asked, "How are things going?"

Rufus looked over at them with a wide smile. "It's all fascinating."

"We've just talked about a few of the skills some people have," Finch explained. "And I explained some history of abilities going back thousands of years. We were just going to start practicing the card exercise." He looked at the men sitting in lawn chairs in front of him. "Miss Courtney has recently mastered this so she will demonstrate."

Courtney took the pack of playing cards from Finch, shuffled them, and handed them back to him. Finch spread the cards on the table and when Courtney pointed to one, the man lifted it from the deck and looked at it.

"Now, Miss Courtney will try to determine the card I'm holding." Finch closed his eyes and concentrated.

Courtney did the same. In three minutes, she opened her eyes. "Okay. I think I have it." She took a deep breath. "You're holding the three of spades."

Without expression, Finch turned the card to face the small audience.

"No way!" Rufus jumped up. "You're kidding us."

Courtney beamed.

"This is a trick to tease us," Tom accused them.

"I assure you, it is no trick," Finch assured the men.

Rufus stared at his girlfriend in awe. "Who knew? This is amazing."

"Can you teach us?" Josh asked.

"We can certainly try. Through practice, if nothing else, you will all become more sensitive to the unseen," Finch said.

"Cool." Rufus sat down again.

The women took the girls and the animals to sit under the pergola away from the teaching session to allow the men to concentrate. Ellie's garden beds were still spilling over with beautiful colorful blooms and the sky was turning pink and blue and lavender as the sun neared the horizon.

They could hear Rufus ask Mr. Finch to teach them about telekinesis and when Finch began his explanation, Ellie looked her sisters in the eye and winked.

After fifteen minutes of instruction about physics, atoms, energy, and forces, Finch asked if one of the men would go inside the house and bring out a teaspoon.

Josh hurried in, returned with the spoon, and handed it to Mr. Finch. Finch placed the object on the table and gave additional explanations about energy and matter.

Rufus stepped up to the table and the older man instructed him on thought, waves, and pressure using the example of sound waves. "Sound waves exist as pressure in air. They are created by an object vibrating which makes the air vibrate. Energy produced by thought will do the same thing." Finch told Rufus to close his eyes and concentrate on creating sound waves.

Rufus scrunched up his eyes and focused.

In a few moments, Tom, Josh, and Jack nearly jumped out of their chairs.

The spoon on the table began to bend, slowly at first, then a little faster as the end of the spoon folded over.

"Look!" Tom shouted to Rufus to open his eyes.

Rufus gasped and stepped backwards, shocked

to see what he'd done. "What the...? I did that?" The blood drained out of the young man's face leaving him looking ashen.

Finch couldn't keep from smiling. "I'm afraid you had some help. Quite a lot of help." The man knew that it was Ellie who had bent the spoon. He gestured to the women under the pergola.

Ellie smiled and waved, and the tension in Rufus's body released.

"Oh, my gosh." Rufus clutched at his chest and laughed. "I almost passed out. Don't ever do that to me again."

22

The sun's afternoon rays felt good against Angie's and Jenna's faces as they stood high on Robin's Point looking out over the ocean. It was a place dear to the sisters' hearts. When they were kids, the Roselands spent many happy summers at the Point with their nana at her cottage until a problem with the land resulted in her losing her cozy, little house. Whenever Angie and her sisters were on the Point, they felt their grandmother was near to them, and they drew strength and resilience from that closeness.

Many years after the residents of the Point lost their houses and before Angie and Josh had met, Josh and his brother purchased the land from the town and had the lovely Sweet Cove resort built on it. When Josh fell in love with Angie, he bought out his brother's ownership share in the resort and had a lawyer draw up papers that returned most of Robin's Point to the Roseland sisters. None of them had built on it, and they weren't sure if they ever would.

"We need Nana's guidance and strength to help solve these murder cases." When the wind blew some strands of hair into Angie's eyes, she pushed them away from her face and then bent to pat Violet.

"We sure do." Jenna had made a chart of suspects, details, and clues and the family had spent the prior evening together going over the information in a careful, methodical way. Some suspects were eliminated and others had either a star or a question mark placed next to their names, with the star indicating high suspicion and the question mark meaning *maybe*.

"I'm still thinking Rachel's sister could be guilty." Jenna watched Violet sniffing near the edge of the cliff. She was about to call to the dog to come away from the edge, and then realized that if Violet fell, it wouldn't hurt her since she was already a ghost.

"I think so, too. And I keep thinking about the boyfriends, but Chief Martin has eliminated Jason Field because people saw him at the state park at the time of Rachel's disappearance."

"Maybe we're getting close to finding the killer

and we don't even know it." Jenna tried to sound upbeat.

"I hope so. We'd better get going if we want to be at the appointment on time."

The sisters and Violet made the drive to the small town of Eastford on the Massachusetts-New Hampshire state line where Rachel's client had a house she wanted renovated. Rachel and Jessica had met with the woman during the weekend when Rachel was visiting her friend.

Leaving the highway, they drove past rolling hills, meadows, and woodlands on the way to meet the client.

"It sure is pretty here," Jenna noted.

When they saw the mailbox with the number they were looking for, Angie turned the car onto the long, winding driveway and followed it to the house set in an open field surrounded by trees.

When she saw the house, Angie stomped on the brakes and gasped.

Jenna's eyes went wide and Violet stared out the window.

"This is it," Angie whispered.

"It's the farmhouse from Mr. Finch's painting." Jenna's mouth hung open as she turned to her sister. "Is the owner the killer?"

"Let's go find out." Taking in a deep breath to help calm her surprise, Angie moved the car forward and parked in front of an old barn. As they were getting out of the car, a woman walked around from the side of the old house.

Lynette Montrose was forty-one, very slim, and had short curly blond hair. She'd made her fortune from a national chain of boutiques and a makeup line she created.

"Hello." Lynette shook hands with the sisters. "I'm Lynette."

"Thanks for meeting with us." Angie introduced herself and Jenna.

"You're helping the police investigate the murders of those two women?"

"We are. We do interviews and research for them."

Lynette nodded. "Would you like to see the house before we talk?"

"That would be great. How did you select Rachel Princeton to do the renovation design?" Angie walked next to Lynette and Jenna as they headed for the house.

"I did a good deal of research and Rachel consistently was rated at the top. She had terrific ideas, things I never thought about. She really considered the use of the rooms, how important sunlight and open spaces are to me. She was coming up with the perfect mix of pleasing aesthetics yet maintaining the historic nature of the place. I'll walk you around the outside of the house first."

As they walked, Lynette pointed to architectural details of the house and explained where the rooms were located.

"This belonged to my grandparents years ago. When I found out it was on the market, I bought it sight unseen. I knew it would require extensive renovations, and I was right. And then, this happened."

They walked around the corner to the rear of the farmhouse to see the ell built off the rear of the home. It was charred, windows had blown out, and one wall looked like it might collapse. Violet ran closer and sniffed at the burnt wood.

"What happened?" Angie asked.

"Arson. I live in Boston and I'm not here much. Somebody thought it might be amusing to burn down an abandoned building. Only it isn't abandoned." Lynette crossed her arms over her chest. "Luckily, it was discovered quickly and the firefighters put it out fast. Otherwise, I could have lost the whole house."

"Was the arsonist caught?" Jenna questioned.

"Not yet. I assume it was some teens looking for trouble." The woman shrugged. "What's done, is done. Now I need to focus on the renovation. I really need a new architect now. I want to get things started so the ell won't be open to the elements once the winter sets in. I also will be mounting security cameras and lights around the periphery as well as inexpensive fire sprinklers inside. They'll have to be removed when the rebuild starts and replaced when it's finished, but I'm not going to chance losing the house. I also have a caretaker who checks on it several times a day."

"It seems you've done all you can to prevent any more damage," Angie told the woman.

"If the arsonist is found, I'll file charges and have him prosecuted to the fullest extent of the law."

After the outside tour was finished, Lynette showed them the interior of the farmhouse. The ell was off limits and had to be avoided due to the extensive damage done by the fire.

The house was built in 1799 and had several additions completed over the decades. It had four-teen rooms and beautiful details in each of them.

"I'm grateful it was only the ell off the back of the house that sustained damage," Lynette said. "It would break my heart to have the main part of the home destroyed."

After the tour was completed, the woman suggested they sit outside since the house had no furniture in it. She'd put a few lawn chairs on the grass near the barn and they settled down to talk.

Violet had been sniffing around the barn and yard and came over to join the women.

"How can I help?" Lynette asked.

"You asked to see Rachel about the renovation when she was visiting her friend in New Hampshire?" Angie started the questioning.

"I got in touch with her because I was here unexpectedly. I'd been in New York City for two weeks straight on business and some things got canceled so I came up here to the house. If she was available, I thought we should take the opportunity to meet. She was nice enough to agree to my request."

"Jessica came with Rachel?" Jenna asked.

"She did. She sat in the car most of the time, but she did walk around the outside and the inside with us. When Rachel and I were discussing the details, Jessica went to wait in the car. Rachel came up with some ideas that really impressed me."

"Had you met Rachel prior to that day?"

"Oh, yes. Many times. She was a lovely woman."

"Was anyone else here that day?"

"No, just me and Rachel. And her friend."

"How did Rachel seem?"

Lynette said, "Professional, personable, accommodating. The same as every other time I'd met her."

"She didn't seem nervous or distracted or anything like that?" Jenna asked.

"I didn't notice anything unusual in her behavior or demeanor. She seemed normal."

"Did you happen to notice anyone watching the house while Rachel was here?"

Lynette rubbed her hands over her arms. "Now you're scaring me. I didn't see anyone lurking around." The woman leaned forward in her chair. "You don't think the murders are linked to the arson, do you? What link could there possibly be? Why would a killer connect the two women to me? We had a simple meeting here. It didn't last long."

Angie attempted to reassure Lynette. "No, no. I only asked if you noticed anyone around because we wondered if Rachel and Jessica were being watched."

Violet turned to look at Angie.

"I see," Lynette said. "That's a relief."

"Are you married?"

"No, I'm not. I've been divorced for a long time."

"Do you have a partner or a close friend who is involved in the renovation?"

"Not at all. The house belongs solely to me. No one else is involved. My long-time partner and I parted ways about two months ago. Amicably, I might add. Things just weren't working out between us. He was busy with his business and I'm busy with mine. We parted as friends. So no, there's no one else who has anything to do with this house." She smiled. "That actually makes it a lot easier ... no one else's opinion to deal with."

The sisters finished the interview and thanked Lynette for her time.

"Call me if you need to ask any more questions."

They walked to the car with Violet beside them, and as Angie was driving down the long driveway, Jenna asked, "There's no connection between the murders and the fire, huh?"

"I only said that so we didn't alarm Lynette. There's definitely a connection. We just have to find it."

23

Driving down the main street of Eastford on the way to the highway, Jenna asked, "Want to stop and get a bite to eat? Suddenly, I'm starving."

"Fine with me. Anyplace look good?" Angie slowed the car a little.

"There's a diner ahead. *Open all day* it says. How about that place?"

"Sounds great." Angie found a space to park right on the street and she maneuvered the vehicle into the spot.

They walked down to the diner with Violet trotting along with them, and the waitress brought them to a booth with windows looking out to the street.

"I want pancakes, with bananas and strawberries

... and whipped cream," Jenna said after looking over the menu. "I didn't eat any lunch today."

Angie smiled. "So that means you can go wild."

"Yup. What are you having?"

Angie chuckled as she patted Violet who was sitting next to her in the booth. "Same as you."

When the stacks of buttermilk pancakes arrived, the sisters' eyes went wide. The huge plates held the tower of pancakes smothered in a generous heaping of berries and bananas with a crown of whipped cream.

"Oh, gosh." Jenna looked sheepish. "We should have split one order."

"We can bring home the leftovers." Angie added a bit of maple syrup and dug in.

"*If* there are any leftovers," Jenna kidded. "What did you think of Lynette?"

"She seemed forthcoming and open. I didn't pick up on anything to indicate she had some reason to kill Rachel and Jessica."

"I thought the same thing." Jenna looked at the dog. "What did you think, Violet?"

The dog wagged her shimmering tail.

"Okay then, we're all in agreement. Lynette doesn't belong on the suspect list."

"Her place was the target of arson," Angie

pointed out. "What's going on with that? We both think the fire has something to do with the murders."

"Definitely," Jenna said. "But why, how, and who are up in the air."

"What could the connection be? Let's brainstorm."

Jenna paused her eating of the pancake tower. "Whoever committed the crimes was after Rachel, Jessica, and Lynette?"

"Makes sense." Angie put down her fork. "But what would tie them together? I doubt Rachel or Jessica knew Lynette socially. Lynette hired Rachel to do the renovation design work. Is that enough of a connection to instigate the crimes that someone has committed?"

"I'd say *no* to that." Jenna sipped her coffee.

"Then what in the world did someone have against the three women?"

"Neither of them was killed because of the other women. I mean like collateral damage." Jenna thought about the situation. "Both women were alone when the killer struck and Lynette wasn't even at the farmhouse. The arsonist must have known she wasn't there. The killer-arsonist deliberately attacked the women, or in Lynette's case, attacked

her house. He went after each one in a very delib-
erate fashion."

"That means the killer has animosity towards all
three women," Angie acknowledged.

"Chief Martin will be interested in what we
learned today. Maybe it will help him figure this
out," Jenna spoke with a hopeful tone.

A young woman entered the diner, saw Angie
facing her from the booth, and waved.

"Amy Windfall just came in." Angie nodded to
the door.

Amy approached the booth. "Hey, how are you?
What a coincidence. I'm meeting a friend for an
early dinner. Did you meet the woman who owns
the house Rachel was designing the renovation for?"

"We did. We just came from there," Angie
told her.

"Is your friend here?" Jenna asked. "Want to sit
with us until they show up?"

"Oh, sure. That would be nice." Amy slid in next
to Jenna.

From her spot in the booth next to Angie, Violet
looked the woman over.

"Are you making any progress on the case?" Amy
asked.

"We learn more each day. Hopefully, the police

are getting closer." Angie wished that was actually the truth.

"After you left the other day," Amy said, "I remembered something I should probably have told you. I was going to call you about it."

Angie's senses perked up and she couldn't help but lean a little closer, unable to hide her keen interest. "What was that about?"

"You know I told you Rachel and Jess went out to that farmhouse the weekend Rachel was up here for a visit? Well, Jess said she left her phone at the house and didn't realize it until Lynette Montrose called Rachel to let them know. Lynette owns those well-known high-end fashion stores. She has a makeup line, too. I tried some of her products. I thought they were really good. That woman is so wealthy. I don't know why she has an old house in this tiny town. Anyway, Jess and Rachel were in the car heading back to Hollis when Lynette called. Jess wanted her phone so they turned around. Lynette told them she was leaving to drive back to Boston, but she'd leave the phone in the milk box on the front porch near the door."

"Did something happen when they went back?" Jenna wished Amy would get to the point.

"That's the weird thing," Amy said. "They pulled

into the driveway. Jess said it was a very long driveway and it was really dark. She parked the car facing the porch since there weren't any lights. She was going to use the headlights to find the milk box on the porch. Rachel got out, too, and they practically ran to the door. Jess said it was scary out there in the dark. She found the milk box and her phone was in it like Lynette said it would be. Here's the really creepy part."

Amy paused for a breath. "When they were hurrying down the porch steps, they almost smacked right into a man who was heading for the front door."

"Who was it?" Angie's heart was pounding.

"They didn't know, but Jess told me he growled at them. He asked why they were trespassing. Rachel explained why they were there. Jess said the guy seemed like he didn't believe them. He threatened to call the police. They explained again their reason for being at the house. Jess said they were both afraid of the man. She told me he shouted at them in a very intimidating way and told them to get out of there and not to come back."

"Did he say who he was? Why he was there?" Jenna asked.

"He didn't. They had no idea who he was." Amy

shook her head. "Could it have been the caretaker or someone like that? He must have thought they were going to break into the house."

"That could be." Jenna nodded. "He must have wanted to scare them so they didn't come back."

"Did they say what the man looked like?" Angie asked.

"They couldn't really tell. It was dark. The headlights backlit the guy. Jess said he was a little taller than average. He wore a baseball hat. That's all she said about his appearance. It was dark, it was hard to see his face, and they were scared and just wanted to get out of there."

"Did Jess or Rachel tell Lynette about the man? Did they get an answer as to who he was?" Angie questioned.

"Jess didn't call her. I don't know if Rachel told her about what happened or not. Jess was embarrassed by the incident. The guy scared her and she didn't know what to do. She had her phone and she wasn't ever going back there anyway, but I guess one of them should have talked to Lynette about it."

Amy looked toward the front door and waved, and then she slid out of the booth. "Here's my friend. Nice talking to you. Good luck with the case." She hurried away to meet her friend.

Angie and Jenna stared at one another.

"What the heck was that about?" Jenna frowned. "Do you think it was the caretaker who scared them?"

"Or someone casing the place? Look around, see what's there. Then go back and set the place on fire?" Angie rubbed at her neck. "So many weird loose threads. How do they form a picture? How do they link together?"

"More information to share with the chief." Jenna leaned back. "When are all these details going to come together and point at the killer?"

"Soon, I hope. Let's go out to the car. I want to call Lynette." Angie paid the bill and they left the diner.

In the car, she placed the call and when Lynette picked up, Angie put it on speaker and then explained about the man at the farmhouse and how Jessica and Rachel were afraid of him.

"Could it have been the caretaker?" Angie asked.

"It could have been. Maybe he thought they were up to no good and wanted to put a scare into them," Lynette said. "I really don't know him that well. He came recommended from a friend of a friend. His name is Peter Moss. I'll give you his number if you want to call him." She looked it up and gave it to Angie.

"What about your ex-partner?" Angie asked. "Might he have gone to the farmhouse to see if you were there? Could it have been him? Maybe Jessica and Rachel startled him and he thought they were planning to break in."

"I don't think it was Tom," Lynette told them. "But who knows? He owns the luxury car dealership in Nashua. His name is Tom Boss. He changed his phone number recently and I don't have the new one. You could call the dealership. He's usually there. He lives in Nashua. Why do you want to talk to him?"

"If he was the one who spoke to Rachel and Jessica that night, I'd like to ask if he noticed anything that seemed out of the ordinary. Maybe someone was following Rachel and Jessica," Angie shared.

"Do you know anyone else it could have been?" Jenna asked the woman.

"Really, I don't. If I think of someone, I'll get back to you," Lynette offered.

When the call ended, Angie looked at her sister. "Want to make a quick trip to Nashua? It's only about twenty minutes away."

"You bet I do." Jenna looked at the dog. "How about you, Violet?"

The ghost dog wiggled and wagged her tail.

"It's unanimous." Angie started the car and headed for the highway.

24

Forty-three-year old Tom Bass, the dealership owner, was about five feet ten inches tall, fit-looking with broad shoulders, dark hair, and blue eyes. When he smiled, he showed prefect rows of bright white teeth.

"Hello," the man called to them after being told by a salesperson two women would like to speak with him. "I'm Tom Bass. How can I help you?"

Angie made introductions and before giving her short speech about being police consultants investigating two homicides, she noticed an unusual skull ring on Tom's finger. She also noticed he wore a diamond earring on one earlobe. She wondered if some of his older customers would be put off by his jewelry choices, but if they were, it clearly didn't impact his success. His dealerships were always ranked at the top for sales in two states.

Violet kept her eyes glued to the businessman.

Tom's face lost its smile. "Come into my office." He gestured for Angie and Jenna to walk inside with him.

The dealership was the typical glassed-walled building where potential customers could easily look in through three sides to see the gleaming new vehicles proudly displayed in the showroom. Tom's spacious office was on the second floor with two floor-to-ceiling glass walls. Expensive and classy furniture had been chosen to project the success of the man who occupied the office. Framed photos of Tom with sports stars, politicians, and local celebrities hung on the wall behind the desk and various community awards were displayed on the credenza.

"Please have a seat." Tom moved to the seating area by the windows where he took a club chair while the sisters sat on the pale gray sofa. Violet sat by the windows and watched the man. "What can I help with?"

Angie asked him straight out. "Were you at Lynette Montrose's farmhouse in Eastford one evening recently?"

Tom blinked at the young woman for a few

seconds. "I stopped by the farmhouse to see if Lynette was there. I'd been in Boston and was driving home and decided to detour over to the house."

"Why did you want to see Lynette?" Jenna questioned the man with a pleasant tone.

Tom squared his shoulders and smiled. "Lynette and I ended our relationship not long ago. We were together for years. Our split was friendly. I still care about her. I was hoping to see her and chat. I also wanted to hear about how the renovation design was coming along."

"And was she at the house?"

"She wasn't."

"Did you happen to run into anyone else while you were there?" Angie kept her focus on the emotions Tom was giving off.

The man tilted his head slightly with a questioning look in his eyes. "I did. Two women were trespassing. How did you know about that? Have there been other incidents in the area?"

Angie ignored his questions. "Can you tell us what happened when you ran into the women?"

"Sure." Tom appeared eager to help. "I saw a car parked near the house when I came down the driveway. The house is set quite far back from the road and has a long, winding driveway leading to the house and barn. I parked near the barn, got out, and headed for the house just as they came down the porch steps. I was alarmed that they were trespassing so I called them out. They told me they had met with Lynette earlier and one of them had left her phone behind. They came to collect it. I wasn't sure about the story they were telling me. Anyone could make that up." Again he asked, "Have those two been seen trespassing in other places?"

Jenna spoke with a somber voice. "The two women were murdered recently."

Tom sat straight, his face showing alarm. "Murdered?" His eyebrows raised and his eyes shifted to the windows for a few moments. "Was one of them the young woman from Hollis?"

"Yes, she was one of the victims," Angie told him. "The other was an architect who lived in Sweet Cove."

"I'm shocked. What they told me about why they were at Lynette's house was the truth? I didn't believe them." Tom looked from Jenna to Angie. "How do you know they were the ones at the farmhouse? I mean, they aren't alive to tell anyone they were there."

"They did tell some people … before they were murdered."

"I was a little harsh when I spoke to them that night, but I honestly thought they were up to no good." Tom ran his hand over his face.

"Did you happen to see anyone lurking around out on the road near the driveway?" Jenna asked.

Tom looked off into space trying to remember. "I don't think so. I didn't notice anything like that."

"Was anyone walking along the road? It's quite a narrow lane," Angie pointed out. "If someone was walking in the dark, you would have had to move to the middle of the road to avoid them."

"I just don't recall." Tom shook his head with a frown on his face. "I'm sorry I'm not more help."

Angie looked over at the dog to see her staring at Tom.

Tom said, "Lynette isn't being targeted, is she?"

"Why do you ask that?" Jenna held the man's eyes with hers.

"Because the two victims were at Lynette's house, and then the farmhouse was hit by an arsonist. Is Lynette in danger? Is the killer after Lynette?"

"Every detail is being looked into," Angie said. "You'll probably be contacted soon by Chief Phillip

Martin of Sweet Cove. He'll be following up with you."

"Of course. I'm happy to speak with him. Have you talked with Lynette? Does she know to be careful, to be on guard?"

"We have spoken with Lynette," Angie informed the man. "She strikes me as a very smart woman."

"Good. Maybe I'll give her a call after we finish."

Back in Sweet Cove, Angie and Jenna sat in the Victorian's sunroom with Mr. Finch while holding their daughters on their laps and taking turns reading books to Gigi and Libby. The cats and Violet were curled on a rug in front of the fireplace listening to the stories. When both little girls had dozed off, the books were set aside, and Finch asked for more details about Tom Bass.

"He was very friendly, professional, and personable," Angie said. "He admitted to running into Rachel and Jessica at Lynette's the night they returned to the farmhouse to retrieve the phone."

Jenna pushed a strand of hair from Libby's forehead. "He was sure they were trespassing and he gave them a hard time."

"The man was forthcoming then," Finch nodded.

"He was, but I didn't like him," Angie said. "Maybe it was just his salesman vibe. His friendliness seemed forced. I felt like he was dying to sell me a car."

"I felt the same way." Jenna stroked her sleeping daughter's cheek.

"And what did our dog sense?" Finch glanced over to Violet and the dog lifted her head and looked at the man.

Angie shifted Gigi on her lap. "Violet was wary of Tom. Even though he was friendly, he was sort of imposing, with broad shoulders, a loud voice. He seemed to suck all the energy in the room into himself."

"I've known people like that," Finch smiled at the dog.

Euclid stood, went over to Violet, and gently nudged her glimmering body with his nose as if he were trying to protect her.

"My fine orange boy." Finch praised the enormous cat, and Euclid trilled at him.

"Is something wrong, Mr. Finch?" Jenna questioned. "You look a little tired."

The man gave Jenna a kind, caring look. "I have … a feeling."

"Uh oh. What sort of feeling?" Shivers of unease raced over Angie's skin and she held Gigi closer.

"The end of the case is coming."

"And will the ending be a good one or a bad one?" Worry showed in Jenna's eyes when she asked the question.

"That is yet to be determined." Finch paused before he spoke again. "We must all be alert, pay attention to our surroundings. Whatever happens, we will act with purpose."

Josh and Tom came into the room and sat down.

"Kitchen cleanup is complete," Tom announced. "And a fine job was done, if we do say so ourselves."

"Why do you all look so gloomy?" Josh studied their faces.

"The case will be coming to end soon," Angie shared the news.

"That's a good thing." Tom's upbeat expression changed when he saw no one looked pleased. "Isn't it?"

"Hopefully." As Angie tried to ignore her nervousness, she turned to her husband, and took his hand. "Everything will be all right."

Josh held her hand tight in his.

After a minute or two of quiet, Angie said to

Finch, "Have you done any more work on your painting?"

"Some." Finch held his cane between his knees and turned it unconsciously.

"I think I'd like to look at it again."

"You are welcome to see it any time you wish to."

"How about now?" Angie met Finch's gaze.

Tom and Josh lifted their sleeping daughters from their wives' arms and held them to their chests. Angie reached over and helped Finch up from the sofa, and with the cats and Violet slowly leading the way, the small parade walked through the Victorian to the family room at the back of the house and into Finch's apartment.

25

Angie, Finch, and Violet went into the sunroom and stood in front of the painting of the farmhouse while the others stayed in the living room.

"I won't mention what I added or changed. I'll sit here with you while you take a look." Finch sat down on the sofa and picked up a book.

Taking a deep breath, Angie took a step closer to the easel. When she looked at the painting, she felt she was back in Eastford standing outside of Lynette's house. The vibrant colored leaves in the trees, the gorgeous blue of the sky, the handsome antique Colonial. But slowly, the sun faded and the day turned to night.

Angie felt cold standing in the dark outside the farmhouse. Suddenly, her nostrils filled with the acrid, nauseating odor of gasoline, and in a few moments, a flash of orange and red lit up the night with a whoosh and a roar.

She could see flames engulfing the walls of the ell at the back of the farmhouse. The heat was so intense, she wanted to step back, but her feet wouldn't move. The skin on her face was hot.

Off in the distance, she noticed a dark figure running away. She tried to yell to him, but the words only stuck in her throat.

Something moved around her, but it was elusive and her eyes couldn't lock onto it.

The dark night pressed down on her, surrounded her, and then her vision dimmed, and went black.

Angie gasped and saw Mr. Finch standing beside her, his hand on her arm.

"You're all right, Miss Angie. It's me. You're here with me."

After sucking in a breath of air, the young woman blinked and ran her hand over her eyes. "I was back at the farmhouse. The smell of gasoline made me feel ill. The ell was on fire, just like in your painting."

Finch raised a bushy eyebrow. "There is no fire in the painting, Miss Angie."

"Yes, there is." She pointed to the ell on the canvas, and then her arm dropped. "Oh, there isn't. It was only in my mind." Her shoulders slumped. "Something was moving around me, but I couldn't make out what it was. Maybe I should stare at the painting again. Maybe then I could see what I couldn't the first time."

"I don't think so." Finch patted her arm. "That's enough for one night. You don't want to push yourself. Let the images come to you in their own time."

Angie gave the man a soft smile. "We need to tell the images to stop taking so long to tell me something."

"Maybe they can hear us," Finch returned her smile.

Violet rubbed against Angie's legs and she patted the dog's head. "It's okay. I'm fine."

Josh stood in the doorway with worried eyes. "Are you okay, hon?"

"I'm fine." She reached her hand to him and Josh came into the sunroom and gave her a hug.

"Why don't we all head to our rooms and relax for a while," Josh suggested.

Angie hugged Finch. "We'll get to the bottom of it. I think Courtney should have a look at the painting. She's been able to see things in your artwork before."

"I'll speak to her about it." Finch gave a nod. "I'll say goodnight to all of you."

"Sleep well, Mr. Finch," Angie told him.

Later when Gigi and Josh were sound asleep, Angie crept into their living room to join Violet on the sofa for a while. It had become a nightly ritual with the two of them snuggling together while Angie talked about the case.

"Why are my powers so slow this time?" She scratched behind Violet's ears. "I thought my powers were supposed to increase after having Gigi. Well, they seemed to when we were investigating our mom's death. I wish they didn't fade at times. It seems they should stay stable, but what do I know?"

Violet sat next to Angie and listened while she articulated her thoughts.

"It bothers me that Jason Field was removed from the suspect list. Some people in the park told the chief they saw Jason there at the time of Rachel's disappearance, but what if they're lying? What if Jason paid them to lie?"

Angie went on. "And what about Rachel's sister? She has a gambling problem, she's always resented her sister, she was always borrowing money from

248

Rachel. It seems very possible that Rebecca *did* stop at Rachel's house, talked to her about another loan, and when Rachel refused, Rebecca killed her. She took back roads to get to Sweet Cove that day and she had her phone turned off. So she couldn't be tracked. I'm still suspicious of her."

After massaging at the kinks in her shoulders, Angie continued with her monologue. "Tom Bass was at the farmhouse the night Rachel and Jessica returned to fetch the phone. He thought they were trespassing. He claimed not to see anyone lurking nearby ... someone who might have been watching the young women, waiting for the right moment to pounce."

Angie ran her hand over the ghost dog. "We're sure taking a long time to figure this out," she told Violet. "I bet you want to go back to wherever you were before you came here. If you need to return, we'll keep working on it. We won't give up."

Angie didn't want the dog to leave, but she knew she couldn't stay. Euclid had been sleeping in Gigi's room, and Circe had been on the bed with Josh. Both felines padded into the living room and jumped up on the sofa to sit with Angie and Violet. Each cat touched noses with the dog before settling down.

"My two best cats," Angie smiled and patted them. "Everything's going to be okay."

When Angie was getting ready to close the bake shop the next day, Chief Martin walked in and took a seat at the counter.

"Coffee?" Angie brought him a black coffee. "How are things?"

"About the same." The chief took a long drink. "I went to talk to Tom Bass."

"Did you learn anything?"

"Not much. He was very cooperative. Was willing to do what he could to help the investigation. Similar to how he was when you and Jenna spoke with him. He gave the same answers."

"I don't like that he just showed up at the farm-house," Angie scrunched her forehead in thought. "Why did he think Lynette would be there? Why didn't he call her first to see if she was at the house?"

"All good questions. He told me he was in the area and didn't want to pull to the side of the road to make the call. He was nearby so he decided on the spur of the moment to drive over there."

"Who knows if that's the truth?" Angie grumped. "What kind of a car does he drive? Is it an F-150?"

The chief smiled. "The man owns several car dealerships. He drives whatever he wants, whenever he wants."

"Right." Angie put her elbow on the counter and set her chin in her hand.

"As far as Rachel's sister ... the techs have been working on the phone. Even though a phone is turned off, signals are still being sent from it. The techs report that the phone was in Sweet Cove, but they haven't been able to pinpoint if Rebecca was near her sister's place."

"And what about Jessica's ex-boyfriend? He called her when he was drunk and was verbally abusive to her."

The chief said, "He's a jerk. Not sure yet if he's a murderer."

"Things are moving slowly," Angie sighed. "What are we going to do?"

"Keep plugging." The chief finished his coffee and set the mug on the counter.

"Mr. Finch thinks something is going to happen soon."

"I hope he's right. The sooner, the better."

"He means something dangerous. So be careful."

Chief Martin's expression tensed. "That's good to know. I have to get to a meeting. Watch your back, Angie. Call me if you need anything."

"I will."

Angie finished up the end-of-day tasks, took her apron off and put it in the laundry bin, then went into the Victorian and to the kitchen. She wanted a nice, hot shower and then, a bite to eat. There was a note on the kitchen island for her.

Tom and Josh took the kids to the park. Ellie went to the market and Mr. Finch is at the candy store. I'm heading there now. Jenna's working in her shop. I looked at Mr. Finch's painting. It was weird. Everywhere I looked at the picture, I could see a tiny, little skull. He hadn't painted it. I just imagined they were there. Sorry I wasn't more help with it. See you later. Love, Courtney.

She'd drawn two little hearts near her signature that made Angie smile.

Angie looked around for the cats and Violet, but the kitchen was empty so she headed for the hall that led to Jenna's jewelry store and workshop.

She stopped short, thinking about the little skulls Courtney saw in the painting.

Then she heard a dog bark, and a wave of anxiety washed over her like a tidal wave.

Violet rarely barks. Who was that?

Angie ran down the hall. "Jenna?"

When she opened the door to the workshop, she saw Jenna tied to a chair near the fireplace. There was a gag over her mouth and her face was full of fear.

Angie turned and saw what had frightened her sister.

Tom Bass stood near the backdoor ... with a huge knife in his hand.

"Shut that door behind you." He pulled a chair out from the work table and placed it in the middle of the room. "Sit."

Angie didn't move. "What are you doing? What are you doing here?"

"Tying up loose ends. Take a seat."

Angie could smell gasoline. She looked around the room and saw the gas can on the floor.

"I heard there's an arsonist around here somewhere." Tom smiled an ugly smile. "Sit."

Angie's blood boiled. If she sat, she knew what would happen to them. "No."

Tom's face darkened. "Either sit or I'll cut your throat."

Angie saw something sparkling behind the man.

"Come and do it then," she taunted Tom.

His face turned red with rage, and as he started

forward, Euclid crashed through the window screen near Jenna's desk, skidded across the top of the workspace, and jumped down to the floor. Circe was right behind him.

Tom stopped his advance on Angie and spun around.

Violet's particles glowed red and intensely bright, and she charged at the man, barking loud and wild, then bit into his leg and held on. The cats flung themselves at Tom, hung onto him with their claws, and ferociously bit and scratched at him.

In the chaos, Angie ran to untie Jenna, grabbed the fireplace poker and held it like a bat. She approached the screaming man being attacked by the animals, but the cats and dog were all over him so she couldn't get a swing in without hitting one of them.

Jenna made the emergency call then ran to stand by her sister. "Give me that poker. I want a chance to pummel the monster."

Tom was on the floor, unconscious, by the time the police and EMTs arrived, and the cats were sitting quietly on the loveseat. Violet stood off to the side ready to lunge at the man if he woke up.

One of the paramedics checked Tom's wounds

before they lifted him onto the stretcher. "The cats did this? Looks like dog bites. Weird."

Chief Martin rushed in and let out a sigh of relief when he saw Jenna and Angie, pale and shaky, talking to the officers. He walked over, put an arm around each one, and pulled them into a long hug. When he stepped back, he said, "Looks like I should be hugging the cats, too."

"Yeah," Angie said. "And someone else." She glanced over at Violet sitting in the corner, and smiled.

26

A few days later, Chief Martin met with the sisters and Finch to discuss some findings of the case.

"Employees and associates of Tom Bass said he'd been acting erratically since he and Lynette ended their relationship. Tom had confided in one person he worked with that he'd attempted to get back together with Lynette, but that she wasn't open to the idea and wanted to remain friends. The man Tom told this to reported that Tom went on a rant against Lynette. It was behavior he'd never seen before in his boss."

"Tom sure acted like it was an amenable parting of the ways when we saw him at the dealership," Jenna said.

"He put on a good front most of the time, but it

seems the man was slowly crumbling mentally," the chief told them. "This next bit of information must remain confidential as the investigation is ongoing and could impact the outcome of a trial should the material get out." The chief took in a long breath and continued. "Tom's computer was seized and the techs found some unpleasant stuff on it. It seems Tom was planning to abduct Lynette, torture her, and burn the farmhouse down with her in it."

Everyone in the room gasped.

"There were documents on his laptop where he wrote extensively about his rage and all the wrongs done to him by Lynette. He'd written about how he ran into Rachel and Jessica at the farmhouse. How he followed them back to New Hampshire to Jessica's house. Tom's plan was to break in and kill both of them, but when he arrived at the house, some friends were just going inside so he had to abort the mission. He believed he had to murder the women so they couldn't report to the police they'd seen him at Lynette's house. He was the one who set fire to the place. He was the one who sent the threatening notes to Rachel. There were copies of the notes on his laptop. Tom followed Rachel back to Sweet Cove and killed her a couple of days later. He tried several times to attack Jessica, but something always thwarted his attempt, until he finally gained access to her house and ended her life."

"How terrible." Ellie shook her head. "The man had lost his mind."

"Tom is in the hospital right now. A psychologist will be determining if he can stand trial or not. Otherwise, the plea will be insanity."

"Does Lynette know what Tom did ... and was planning to do?" Angie asked.

"She does now. She was briefed by a detective who's familiar with the case." The chief looked around the room at everyone. "We also know what he was planning to do when he arrived here. The man had to eliminate anyone who could connect him to either the attempt to burn down the farmhouse or to the murders of Jessica and Rachel. And by trying to cover his tracks, he left more clues behind."

"It's a horrible tale," Courtney sighed. "He'd clearly lost touch with reality."

The day was warm and sunny and the sky was a gorgeous deep blue when the family and friends gathered in the cemetery for the graveside service for Rachel Princeton. Even though they'd never met the woman, the Roselands, Finch, and Chief Martin wanted to pay their respects. Rachel's sister, Rebecca, and a few other members of the family, along with close friends stood near to the casket with everyone else gathering around in a U-shape.

Violet had come with them and sat next to Angie as the minister spoke the prayers, some people gave eulogies, and three musicians played several selections with flute and cellos.

Angie glanced down at the dog and made eye contact with her. She reached down and patted Violet's head.

When the service ended, people mingled and chatted with one another, and the sisters, Finch, and the chief went over to offer condolences to Rebecca who thanked them for their help in solving the case.

As they were about to leave the cemetery, Angie saw Violet perk up. Her ears twitched and her head spun around to stare at the hill leading to the pet graveyard.

Jenna moved closer to her sister. "Look up by the trees near the entrance to the pet cemetery."

Angie followed her sister's gaze to the spot where they'd first seen Violet. Something shimmered in the sunlight, but Angie couldn't make out what it was.

With her tail wagging, Violet trotted toward the hill, but stopped, and looked back at the family.

"What's there?" Angie asked.

"I think it's Rachel Princeton. It's her ghost. She seems to be calling to Violet," Jenna told her.

Angie looked at the dog, and whispered, "Go ahead, Violet. It's all right. It's Rachel."

Violet glanced up the hill, then turned and hurried over to each member of the family. Each person patted the ghost dog and wished her well. Angie was the last one the dog approached.

She bent down. "The crimes are solved. Now you and Rachel can be together again. She's waiting for you."

Violet's nose rubbed against the young woman and then her tongue ran over Angie's cheek.

"Thank you for saving us from Tom Bass. I'll tell Gigi and Libby it was time for you to go, and I'll tell Euclid and Circe you said goodbye." Tears gathered in Angie's eyes. "We'll miss you. Go and be happy together. I love you, sweet Violet."

The dog kept her eyes glued to Angie for another few seconds, then she wagged her tail, and turned around. In an instant, she'd raced up the hill and was bouncing around the glittering particles that were her former owner.

Jenna watched. "Rachel picked her up. She's kissing Violet. I can see her happy tears." Jenna's words caught in her throat and she brushed at her eyes. "Rachel is looking at all of us. She put her hand over her heart. She thanks us."

The shimmering lights at the top of the hill faded and disappeared.

"They're gone," Jenna said softly, and reached for Angie's hand.

"And may they live joyously ever after," Finch smiled.

Because it was a beautiful late Saturday afternoon with unseasonably warm temperatures, the family decided to have a cookout and invited their friends to join them.

"It might be the last cookout of the year," Josh told them as he set up the grill.

"I'm hoping we'll have nice weather through October." Courtney carried over a platter with burgers, marinated chicken breasts, veggie burgers, and Italian sausages, and set it on the table next to the grill. "Here's your grilling apron," she handed one to

Josh. "And here's one for Tom ... the good Tom, not the killer one."

"I like the sound of that. I think I'll have a t-shirt made that says *I'm the Good Tom*."

Courtney chuckled and went back into the house to get more food.

Mr. Finch, Betty, Orla, and Mel were playing corn hole while Rufus was battling Chief Martin and his wife, Lucille at badminton.

After missing a shot, Rufus puffed. "I need Courtney to help me."

Jenna and Angie played with the little girls under the pergola and Euclid and Circe sat in the lawn chair.

"It seems funny not to have Violet around." Angie handed Gigi a toy elephant.

"It sure does," Jenna agreed. "She was already part of the family."

Euclid and Circe trilled.

"Where's Ellie and Jack?" Jenna asked.

"They texted me. They're on their way. They stopped to pick up some beer and wine."

Right on cue, the couple came around the side of the house, wearing wide smiles.

"We have good news," Ellie told the group and

everyone stopped what they were doing and walked over to hear.

Jack's face was flush with happiness. "Our offer on the land has been accepted."

The family members and friends rushed over to hug them and offer congratulations.

"I really didn't think our offer would be accepted." Ellie smiled. "Now the hard part comes. Planning the neighborhood and getting the funding to build it. But we're over one hurdle. We'll do our best to make it happen."

"Such happy news," Finch beamed.

Jack turned to Ellie. "And here's some other happy news." The man knelt on one knee and took Ellie's hand. "You are the best thing that's ever happened to me. Every day is happier, more fun, and more interesting because you're in my life."

Tears streamed down Ellie's face.

"Will you stay with me forever? Will you always be my best friend and my love? Will you marry me, Ellie?"

The tall blond nodded. "Yes. Yes, I will."

Jack took a small velvet box from his pocket and slipped a stunning diamond ring on Ellie's finger. "It was my grandmother's engagement ring."

"It's beautiful."

Jack stood and swept Ellie into his arms for a sweet, loving kiss while everyone else cheered and clapped.

Circe and Euclid threw back their heads and howled with joy.

"I never thought this would happen," Courtney kidded. "They're as slow as molasses."

"I love a wedding," Josh whooped.

"If I'd known this was going to be an engagement celebration," Angie said, "I would have baked a fancy cake."

"We'll make do with all the wonderful desserts you did make," Finch said to Angie as he walked over to Ellie and wrapped her in his arms. "Congratulations to you, my dear." He shook Jack's hand. "And best wishes to you. Welcome to the family. Although, you've been a part of it for years already, this makes it official."

"This calls for a toast," Tom told them.

"There's a bottle of champagne in the bag with the beer and wine," Jack said. "I bought it in case Ellie said *yes*."

Champagne flutes were brought out and filled, and several toasts were offered up until everyone was giddy.

The food was carried to the long table, the

candles and tiki torches were lit, and they all sat together to enjoy the feast.

When the evening was over and everything had been cleaned up and put away, the guests left, and everyone else was in the house, Josh and Angie sat around the fire pit with cups of coffee. Euclid and Circe sat in the Adirondack chairs next to the couple.

"What a happy day." Angie reached for her husband's hand.

"The case is solved, Violet and Rachel have been reunited, Jack and Ellie got the land they wanted, and now they're engaged. Time to plan the wedding." Josh leaned back in his chair.

Angie looked over at the handsome man holding her hand. "I'm not sure how we could be any luckier."

"Or more grateful for all the wonderful people we have in our lives," Josh added, and then looked over at the cats. "And for our two fine felines. We are truly blessed."

Euclid and Circe trilled, stood, and leapt down. Euclid jumped onto Angie's lap and Circe joined Josh in his chair, and the four of them sat together on that beautiful, tranquil September evening, under the sparkling moon and twinkling stars.

THANK YOU FOR READING! RECIPES BELOW!

Books by J.A. WHITING can be found here:
www.amazon.com/author/jawhiting

To hear about new books and book sales, please sign up for my mailing list at:
www.jawhiting.com

Your email will never be sold, shared, or spammed.

If you enjoyed the book, please consider leaving a review. A few words are all that's needed. It would be very much appreciated.

BOOKS BY J.A. WHITING

OLIVIA MILLER MYSTERIES (not cozy)

SWEET COVE COZY MYSTERIES

LIN COFFIN COZY MYSTERIES

CLAIRE ROLLINS COZY MYSTERIES

PAXTON PARK COZY MYSTERIES

SEEING COLORS MYSTERIES

ELLA DANIELS COZY WITCH MYSTERIES

SWEET BEGINNINGS BOX SETS

SWEET ROMANCES by JENA WINTER

BOOKS BY J.A. WHITING & NELL MCCARTHY

HOPE HERRING MYSTERIES

TIPPERARY CARRIAGE COMPANY MYSTERIES

VISIT US

www.jawhiting.com

www.bookbub.com/authors/j-a-whiting

www.amazon.com/author/jawhiting

www.facebook.com/jawhitingauthor

J. A. WHITING BOOKS

SOME RECIPES FROM THE SWEET COVE
SERIES

Recipes

SOFT PRETZELS

INGREDIENTS

1½ cups warm water

1 packet active dry yeast or instant yeast (about 2¼ teaspoons)

¾ teaspoon salt

1 Tablespoon brown sugar

1 Tablespoon unsalted butter (melted)

4 cups all-purpose flour

Sea salt (for sprinkling over the pretzels)

INGREDIENTS FOR BAKING SODA BOIL (this step is optional)

½ cup baking soda

9 cups water

DIRECTIONS

Whisk the yeast into warm water.

Allow to rest for a minute.

Whisk in salt, brown sugar, and melted butter.

Slowly add 3 cups flour. Mix with wooden spoon until dough is thick.

Now slowly add ¾ cup of flour and mix again so dough is no longer sticky. If it still is sticky, add another ¼ cup more flour and mix again.

Place dough on floured surface.

Knead for about 3 minutes and shape dough into a ball.

Cover with a towel and let rest for about 10 minutes.

Preheat oven to 400°F.

Line 2 baking sheets with parchment paper (spray with nonstick spray) OR line the baking sheets with silicone baking mats.

With a sharp knife, cut the dough into sections of about ⅓ cup each.

Roll the dough sections into 20-inch ropes.

Take the ends and bring them together to form a circle. Lift the ends and put one side over the other. Now bring them toward you and press them down into the dough to make the pretzel shape.

DIRECTIONS OPTIONAL BAKING SODA BOIL

(This isn't necessary, but will create a chewier pretzel with a traditional taste).

In a large pot, bring baking soda and 9 cups water to a boil.

Drop 1-2 pretzels into the boiling water for 20-30 seconds, then remove with a slotted spoon. Let water drip off. Place on cookie sheet.

Sprinkle with sea salt.

DIRECTIONS IF YOU DON'T DO THE BAKING SODA BOIL

Brush the pretzels with an egg wash (1 beaten egg and 1 Tablespoon milk) and sprinkle with sea salt.

Bake pretzels for 12-15 minutes until golden brown.

Remove from oven and serve warm with your favorite mustard or a nacho cheese sauce.

Pretzels may be stored for up to 3 days in a zip-lock bag or in a container.

NUTELLA S'MORES PIE

INGREDIENTS

12 graham crackers

2 Tablespoons granulated sugar

½ cup butter, melted

2 cups Nutella spread

1 8-oz container of Mascarpone cheese

¼ teaspoon salt

1 cup heavy whipping cream

2 cups mini marshmallows

Chocolate syrup

DIRECTIONS

Preheat oven to 350°F.

In a food processor, pulse graham crackers and sugar until finely ground.

Add butter and pulse until mixed.

Press the mixture evenly into a greased 9" pie pan.

Bake for 15 minutes. Cool.

Beat Nutella, Mascarpone, and salt until fluffy.

In a separate bowl, beat whipping cream on high until stiff peaks form.

Fold whipped cream into Nutella mixture.

Spread the mixture over the pie crust, cover, and refrigerate for 4 hours.

Sprinkle marshmallows over the chilled pie.

Broil for 1-2 minutes until the marshmallows are golden.

Refrigerate for an hour.

Just before serving, drizzle with chocolate syrup.

MAC AND CHEESE CUPS

INGREDIENTS

8 ounces elbow pasta

4 Tablespoons butter (2 Tablespoons for mac and cheese mixture and 2 Tablespoons for breadcrumb topping)

2 Tablespoons flour

½ teaspoon salt

¼ teaspoon black pepper

1 cup milk

2 cups shredded cheddar cheese

½ cup Italian bread crumbs

SERVE WITH:

Fresh parsley, finely chopped, spread over tops

Marinara sauce

DIRECTIONS

Preheat oven to 425°F.

Place 12 liners in a muffin tin and lightly coat with cooking spray.

Cook pasta according to package directions. Drain pasta and set aside.

In large saucepan, melt 2 Tablespoons butter.

Whisk in flour, salt, and pepper.

Stir until thickened (about 2 minutes).

Slowly add milk, heating until just boiling. Remove from heat and stir in cheese.

Add in cooked pasta and stir to coat. Divide evenly between the muffin cups.

In a small saucepan, melt the remaining 2 Tablespoons butter and stir in bread crumbs.

Spoon over tops of the macaroni in the muffin cups.

Bake 18-20 minutes until bread crumbs are golden brown.

Remove mac and cheese cups from muffin tin and sprinkle with chopped parsley.

Serve warm with marinara sauce for dipping.

APPLE AND SPICE BUNDT CAKE

INGREDIENTS

Butter for the pan

Flour for the pan

3¼ cups flour

1¾ teaspoons baking powder

½ teaspoon baking soda

1 teaspoon salt

2¾ teaspoons ground cinnamon

½ teaspoon ground allspice

¼ teaspoon ground cloves

¾ cup walnuts coarsely chopped

¾ cup dried cranberries

½ cup crystallized ginger, chopped

3 baking apples (Honeycrisp, Golden Delicious,

Pink Lady, Braeburn, or Jonagold), peeled, cored, and cut into ½ inch pieces

    1 cup granulated sugar

    1 cup dark brown sugar

    3 eggs

    1½ cups canola oil

    2 teaspoons vanilla extract

Make cinnamon-sugar for sprinkling = 1 Tablespoon granulated sugar and 1 teaspoon cinnamon

DIRECTIONS

Preheat oven to 350°F.

Butter a 10" Bundt pan, dust with flour, tap out the excess.

In a bowl, whisk together flour, baking powder, baking soda, salt, cinnamon, allspice, and cloves.

In another bowl, combine walnuts, cranberries, ginger, and apples.

In a third bowl, combine granulated sugar and brown sugar.

Using an electric mixer on medium-high speed, beat the eggs for one minute.

Add in the oil and beat for one minute.

Add half the sugar mixture, beat one minute, then add the remaining sugar mixture with the vanilla and beat for two minutes.

Scrape down the sides of the bowl with spatula.

With the electric mixer on low speed, add flour mixture, one third of it at a time. Scrape the sides of the bowl after each addition.

Remove bowl from mixer stand. Use a large spoon to stir in apple mixture.

Spoon the batter into the Bundt pan and smooth the top with the spatula. Tap the pan on the counter 2-3 times to settle air pockets.

Bake for 65-70 minutes or until a skewer or toothpick inserted into the cake comes out clean or with only a few crumbs on it.

Set the pan on a rack to cool - about 15 minutes.

Turn the cake out and sprinkle with cinnamon-sugar.

Cool completely.

Cut into slices and serve.

AUTUMN FRUIT PIE

INGREDIENTS FOR CRUST

1 cup all-purpose flour

¼ teaspoon salt

4 Tablespoons cold unsalted butter – cut into 8 pieces

⅓ cup shredded sharp white cheddar cheese

1 Tablespoon granulated sugar

1 egg yolk

4 Tablespoons ice water

INGREDIENTS FOR FILLING

1 stick butter

3 Granny Smith apples

2 Golden Delicious apples

2 D'Anjou pears (better if a little hard)

7 ounces fresh or frozen cranberries

½ cup granulated sugar

1 cup brown sugar

¼ cup all-purpose flour

INGREDIENTS FOR TOPPING

6 Tablespoons softened butter

¾ cup all-purpose flour

½ cup brown sugar

2 teaspoons granulated sugar

Pinch salt

1 teaspoon ground cinnamon

DIRECTIONS FOR CRUST

In a food processor, add flour, salt, cold butter, cold cheese, sugar, and egg yolk and pulse ten to twelve times.

Add four Tablespoons ice water and pulse as you add. Mixture will be crumbly.

Pour the mixture onto a piece of plastic wrap and use the sides of the wrap to pull mixture into a ball. Wrap with the plastic wrap and press into a disc shape. Refrigerate for one hour.

DIRECTIONS FOR FILLING

Peel and core apples and pears and cut into ¼ inch sections.

In a heavy saucepan, melt butter over medium heat.

Add apples and pears to the butter in the saucepan.

Add the cranberries to the saucepan.

Add the sugars and the flour, and stir.

Cover the saucepan and simmer gently for 5 minutes.

Remove cover, gently stir, cook 5 more minutes. Avoid letting mixture stick to the bottom. Mixture should be thick and creamy; the fruit will still be a little hard.

Pour the filling onto a cookie sheet to let cool.

Preheat oven to 425°F.

Dust counter with flour. Roll out the dough – should be 2 inches wider than a 10" deep dish pie plate (2 inches deep).

Place the dough in the pie plate; pinch overhanging dough along the rim, then remove any hanging excess. Flute the edge using thumb and forefinger.

Pour the cooled fruit filling into the pie dish.

DIRECTIONS FOR TOPPING

In a bowl, mix softened butter, flour, sugars, salt, and cinnamon. Spread topping over the filling.

Bake 15 minutes, then lower the oven temperature to 350°F and bake 35-40 minutes or until the fruit is tender when tested with a knife and the top is golden brown.

Cool completely.

Enjoy!

Made in the USA
Middletown, DE
09 August 2023

36432874R00177